# SENSE AND

## *Selected sh*

# by Chris Green

**Also by Chris Green and available on Amazon**

The Early Worm Catches The Bird – *Selected Short Stories*
You Never Can Tell – *Selected Short Stories*
The Black Book and other stories – *Selected Short Stories*

# CONTENTS:

# A Blacker Shade of Blue

Cyan Blue wonders why she is so unhappy. If all the things she is doing are so good for her, she should be in seventh heaven. She gets up at five every morning and does a half an hour's Tai Chi, before her bowl of whole grain cereal with goji berries and manuka honey. She has a healthy outdoor job working with wildlife. She practices yoga, in fact when her friend Indigo is busy, she runs the class for her.

Cyan meditates to a CD with sounds of running water. Her apartment is awash with aloe vera plants to purify the air. She works out at the gym and she takes a veritable orchestra of vitamins and supplements. She cycles everywhere, well nearly everywhere. When she does take the car, she listens to soothing music, Einaudi, Eno or Enya. She never drinks alcohol. She sees Moon two or three times a week. He buys her flowers and they make love tenderly. They go to Inter Faith services on a Sunday. But still she feels her life is empty. Something is missing.

Growing up in Brixton, Jeremy (Jet) Black was beaten up constantly by his big brother, Brad, and he, in turn, hammered his little brother Harry. It was a dog eat dog world where petty crime graduated easily to serious crime. Hierarchies were decided by length of prison sentences. Jet moved swiftly up the hierarchy as he always seemed to be the one who got caught. Since he was sixteen Jet has spent roughly half his life banged up. He is thirty two.

Since his last spell in prison, a two year stretch in Belmarsh for aggravated burglary, Jet has made the decision to go straight. He is tired of the predictable pattern his life has followed, the vicious cycle of get banged up, do his bird, get released, share ideas he learned inside with his crim mates, commit new crimes, get away with things for a bit, get grassed up by one of his crim mates who has already been caught, get nicked, and go back inside. He wants to turn his life around. He is going to avoid *The Black Horse* and *The White Lion* and give *BetterBet* a wide berth. And, he is not going to take back up with Tracey. He can't forgive her for what she said to the police the last time he was arrested. He hadn't laid a finger on her and there he was facing an extra charge of assault. He might otherwise have got away with eighteen months. Now that he is out, he has also decided to stop taking drugs. He has even stopped listening to rap music.

Jet has got himself a part time job at the community centre. At the moment, it is a voluntary position, but Adey, the guy with the pony tail who runs the place, says that if he does a good job there might be an opening. Through a prisoner rehabilitation scheme he has secured a studio apartment in the converted warehouse by the plastics factory. He has started to paint the place with some paint he was given and has discovered a flair for colour. Under the scheme he has also been able to get free items from the furniture project. The bed is a bit rickety and the settee has a few rips, but they will do for now. The microwave works, and that is the main thing. He has been to the animal shelter and got a rescue dog to keep him company, a black and white collie-retriever cross called Bono. He cannot yet afford to join a gym but he has enrolled in a free yoga class. He is not quite sure what yoga is, but he has heard it is very good for you. He has been to one session and although he found it a bit of a struggle he is determined to persevere.

Cyan feels it might help her state of mind if she tried out new things. She needs some excitement to break up the relentless ennui of new age austerity. Something a little reckless, something dangerous, something wild and edgy. She is showing Moon the programme of headline acts for a hard rock festival. Moon is hesitant. He does not like the idea of hard or rock and together, what on earth is she thinking?

'You don't *really* want to go to this, do you?' he says. '*AC/DC* are very loud, you know. And *Anvil Of Doom*. I don't like the sound of them.'

'You only live once,' says Cyan. 'Let's get out there and do something to show we're still alive.'

'But it's all so unwholesome,' says Moon. 'We'd be camping out in a muddy field with hordes of degenerate space cadets and filthy grebos.'

'Not everyone who goes to a festival is a drug addict, Moon' says Cyan.

'*Grim Reaper. Angel Corpse.* Do you really want to see bands with names like that?' says Moon.

'I imagine there are all kinds of new age activities at festivals,' says Cyan. 'Look! It says here. They've got necromancy, neopaganism, tarot divination, and past life regression workshops. And they have a tattoo parlour. I could get some done. They have everything at festivals. The music's probably just an added extra at festivals these days.'

4

'I'm really not sure about the tattoo idea,' says Moon.

'I could have a rose tattooed on my bottom. How about that? I think you'd like that,' says Cyan.

'OK. You win. We'll give it a go,' says Moon. 'But can we go on the Saturday, because I don't want to miss our crystal reading class on Friday.'

'I think we could give crystal reading a miss for once,' says Cyan. 'I haven't got room for any more bloody stones and to be honest I do find Prism's talks a tiny bit boring.'

'Prism? Boring? Surely not, Cyan,' says Moon. 'It's not just about finding out what crystals you need. Don't you remember last week how Prism showed you that your natal chart is a personal treasure map, a dynamic indicator for your soul's path of your healing journey.'

'Well maybe I don't feel very healed,' says Cyan. 'Oh, I don't know, Moon. Perhaps I'm just tired.'

'Let me give you an ayurvedic massage,' says Moon. 'I've got some organic almond oil.'

'I think I'll just have a bath and go to bed,' she says. 'I've got an early start tomorrow. I have a wood to inspect.'

Jet Black is walking Bono in Long Ridge Wood when he spots her. She is the lady who was teaching the yoga class, the one in the flesh coloured leotard who was bent double during the warm up exercises. He would recognise that body anywhere. Not even the Wildlife Trust uniform can hide such a lovely figure. And she has a smile that could bring a dead dormouse back to life.

Cyan recognises him by his tattoos. She knows that she shouldn't, but she does find them attractive. And those muscles. She could tell straight away at the yoga class that although he was lacking in grace, he had been to the gym now and again. She had not seen him though at *Jim's Gym*. Perhaps he was new to town.

'Hello,' he says shyly. He is not used to talking to attractive women. You do not come across many babes in *The Black Horse* or *The White Lion*. And he was certainly protected from such opportunities in Belmarsh. Not even Tracey had been to visit.

'You're not stalking me, are you,' she laughs. 'I've heard about people like you.'

'I'm just taking Bono here for a walk,' he says. 'He loves these

5

woods.'

'Ancient beechwood and unimproved grassland,' she says. 'Maximum biodiversity to provide the basis for a balanced ecosystem.'

'That's a distinctive aroma,' he says, edging a little closer. 'What is it?'

'That will be the rotting leaves,' she says.

'Not that smell,' he says. 'A sweet minty perfume. Is it something that you're wearing?'

'Oh that's patchouli,' says Cyan.

'It's lovely,' he says. 'And so are you.' There! He has said it. There's no going back now.

Moon is not sure what is wrong with Cyan. Something must be troubling her. She said that she is busy at the weekend and now she is not taking his calls. In the two years that they have been seeing each other, nothing like this has happened before. She has always been so accommodating. They have always done everything together. He had hoped they might go to a Channelled Angel Reading on Friday night and then have a snack at *Give Peas A Chance*. Then afterwards they might try out the ginger dusk scented candle, with some soft music. He has called round several times and even spoken to her neighbours but they have not seen her. River who runs the New Age bookshop says he saw her earlier coming out of *BargainBooze* with a big bag, but that can't be right.

Cyan has invited Jet Black round. She has never done such a thing with a stranger before. It is unheard of in the circles she moves in to be so familiar with someone that you've only just met. She is not sure what has come over her. Perhaps it is the rugged profile of Jet's jaw, the pounding testosterone, the rippling muscles and of course the tattoos. Perhaps it is the nascent desire for excitement. Whatever it is, she has never had these kinds of feelings before. She cannot recall ever having strong feelings of any kind. She has always just gone with the flow.

She was brought up in a remote rural location. There was no curriculum at the school she attended and she remained innocent of the ways of the world. She did not rebel as a teenager simply because she was unaware of what she might rebel against. Life was uneventful. There were no highs and no lows. There was no site of struggle in her neighbourhood. In fact, there were no neighbours in her neighbourhood. Her parents did not bother with television which was just as well because a lot of the time there was not even a TV signal in this isolated community. There would probably never be a mobile phone signal.

It wasn't until she went to agricultural college at nineteen that she had her first boyfriend. Dagon was gentle and over a period of several years eased her into intimacy. Inhibited as they both were sex never became the driving force of their relationship. She couldn't understand what all the fuss was about. It was three months before she let Moon over the threshold, and another month before she let him undo the buttons of her blouse. She was in no hurry to move things forward. It wasn't until six months into their relationship that she finally allowed him to explore her panties. She was twenty seven and Moon was only her second lover.

Cyan is on her third glass of wine and feels light headed. She has turned her phone off in case Moon calls again. While she doesn't want to upset him, she does wish he would let her have some space. She had to hide behind the curtain for half an hour earlier. He has gone now. Hopefully, he won't be back until after Jet has had a chance to pin her to the bed, roughly part her thighs and possess her in a frenzy of unbridled passion. Where, she wonders, are these thoughts coming from? What is happening to her?

Something about meeting Cyan has put Jet in touch with his gentler side. He spent the previous evening carving a Buddha from a chunky stick that Bono picked up in the woods. He thinks that the little wooden icon is the sort of thing a girl like Cyan would appreciate; he noticed when they met she wore a Buddha charm bracelet. He has even read a little about Buddha on Wikipedia. Buddha seemed a sound guy, honest and trustworthy and full of thought for others. Not at all like Charlie, the self-styled guru in Belmarsh. Charlie, named after Charlie Manson, Jet found out, would stick a knife in your throat or steal the clothes off your back.

When he arrives at Cyan's though he finds her three sheets to the wind. This is not at all the welcome he was expecting but he has had plenty of experience of this condition with Tracey. It usually ended in a fist fight and the kitchen getting wrecked. While he does not imagine this is going to be the case with Cyan, he needs to tread carefully. He struggles to remember what they were told in the interpersonal psychology class inside. The dude banged on a lot about listening and passivity.

'Would you like a glass of wine,' says Cyan, filling up a tumbler for him from the half empty bottle of Rioja.

'No thanks. I don't drink wine,' says Jet.

'Not even for a special occasion,' she purrs.

Jet remembers the psychology guy saying that distraction was a useful tactic. You could talk someone down who was about to jump or prevent someone with fists raised from hitting you by taking their mind off their subject. 'It's hot and humid in Kuala Lumpur,' he continues. 'It says on the news they are having a heatwave.'

'I've got beer in the fridge,' says Cyan, lurching towards the kitchen.

'I might buy a guitar when I've got some money,' he says. 'And learn to play like George Harrison.'

'I did think of getting some whiskey,' she says. 'I could nip down to the off-licence if you like.'

The psychology guy's reasoning was clearly flawed. 'What I'd really like is a cup of tea,' he says. 'Why don't we both have a nice cup of tea.'

On the way home on the bus, Jet feels despondent. It is clear to him that Cyan has a serious drink problem. He had not suspected this when he met her in the woods. She seemed all sweetness and light then. Perhaps everyone has a deep seated issue if you look for it. At least Cyan is not trying to hide it. She is not a secret drinker like some he has known, Kathy for instance. Kathy would hide it everywhere, under the sink, behind the potted plants, in the garage, in with the grass cuttings, everywhere. He is sure that Cyan is a lovely person beneath it all. He needs to help her. She deserves that much. Helping her will also help him to convince himself that he has changed.

After the embarrassment of the evening though, he decides to leave it a few days and then give her a call. Or maybe wait until he sees her at the yoga class. He will ask if she would like to go for a walk on the common with him and Bono. There are no pubs or retail outlets near the common. She will probably be able to tell him what the trees are and the names of the wildflowers. He could even put together a picnic.

'Why have you been ignoring my calls?' says Moon.

'Can you not shout please,' says Cyan. 'I've got a really bad headache this morning.'

'I'm not shouting,' says Moon. He picks up one of the wine bottles. 'Perhaps you couldn't hear them because of the noise from your party.'

'Sarcasm is just one more thing that you are not very good at,' says Cyan. 'So why don't you just shut up.'

'What's got into you?' says Moon. 'You have not been yourself lately. Is it all to do with me not wanting to go to this rock festival?'

'Why don't you just go off and find a unicorn or a crop circle or something,' says Cyan. 'Just leave me alone, will you?'

Actual Bodily Harm is not the most serious offence in the lexicon of Offences Against The Person. Jet knows that it carries a maximum sentence of five years, but the charge is broad in its scope. It can refer to quite serious injuries, but it can also refer to just a few bruises. Perhaps Cyan and Moon were just pushing each other around a little and Moon fell. Cyan was certainly in a hurry to put a stop to the conversation once she felt that he was prying. But, as Cyan has no criminal record, she will probably just get a fine, he feels, especially if Moon does not want to pursue the matter.

In Jet's experience alcohol is at the root of a majority of threatening behaviour, not just physical aggression but verbal abuse as well. God knows, he had threatened enough people when he had been on the pop and Tracey was at her most vicious after a skinful. Before it lost its licence *The Prince of Wales* on a Friday night could be like Culloden. And, A and E was a who's who of alcoholics after a darts night at *The Caledonian.*

Cyan surely would not have told him to *fuck off and mind his own business* last night when he offered to come round if she was sober. She might be a bit resentful that he didn't respond to her come on the other night and in her booze-fuelled haze have seen it as a rejection. Some people he has heard take rejection very badly. Jet realises that Cyan needs his help more than ever now to turn her life around. He must try to get her off the liquor. An alcohol support group called *NewLeaf* meets at the community centre. When the time is right he will suggest that she goes along.

Cyan does not answer any more of Jet's calls and she is not at the yoga class. He asks Indigo if she might know where she is.

'I haven't seen her,' says Indigo. 'I've phoned her a couple of times but she doesn't seem to be answering.'

'I've been trying to get her all week,' says Jet.

'It's not like her at all,' says Indigo. 'I've known her for years and if she sees that I've called she always gets straight back to me. Do you think perhaps something is wrong?'

'Look. I probably shouldn't say anything but she was arrested last week, says Jet.

'Arrested? Cyan arrested? You're joking, right? she says looking him in the eye. He does not have the look of someone who is joking.

'Yes, for ABH. I think it's all to do with the juice,' says Jet.

'Juice?' says Indigo. 'What do you mean, juice? What kind of juice?'

'You know, the sauce,' says Jet. 'The booze.'

'What?' says Indigo. 'No. Never. Not Cyan. She's about as teetotal as they come. She doesn't even drink tea or coffee.'

'Well, she may not have used to drink,' says Jet. 'But I'm afraid she does now.'

'And I can't imagine her ever being violent,' says Indigo. 'Not in a million years. She wouldn't harm a fly.'

'What about this Moon dude?' says Jet. 'Do you know anything about him?'

'She's been with him for years,' says Indigo. 'Moon's the nicest person you could ever wish to meet.'

'Well, something's gone badly wrong with the universe then,' says Jet.

'You might not be far off with that,' says Indigo. 'There have been some portentous planetary alignments lately. Mercury, Venus, Mars, Jupiter and Saturn were roughly aligned with the Sun ten days ago, and Venus and Mars are in alignment again tonight.'

'There must be a song there somewhere,' says Jet. 'I would like to be able to help Cyan, so if you do hear anything.'

'I know you do. Despite your build and your ..... body art, I can see you are a very sensitive man who is in touch with his feminine side. I could tell as soon as I saw you. You give off a kind vibe.'

His feminine side? This is not something that Jet has been told before. Should he take it as a compliment? Years ago he might have hit anyone who had said this, even if it was a woman. But in the given circumstances, he does feel strangely flattered.

'Why don't you come along to my Vipissana meditation class on Thursday,' says Indigo. 'I think you'd love it.'

'I might just do that,' says Jet, studying Indigo's flesh coloured leotard. 'I think mediation might be exactly what I need.'

Cyan is with her solicitor, Ray Crooner, a thickset man in his forties wearing a dark blue pinstripe suit that is a size too small and a tattersall check shirt. Ray has the pallor of a world-weary defence solicitor and his office has that solicitor's office smell, an odd mix of musk, laser printer toner and disappointment.

'It would not be so bad if you hadn't gone round to your friend Moon's and beat him up all over again,' says Ray. 'He is out of hospital now, I believe.'

Cyan nods.

'We will have to put in a guilty plea and claim mitigating circumstances, but I don't think that you will avoid a custodial sentence. All we can do is try to limit this to three or six months,' he says. 'What would you say we could use as mitigation? Did he hit you? Did he provoke you in any way?Did he crash your car or jump up and down on your iphone or anything that might warrant retaliation? '

'He said that he didn't like my tattoos,' says Cyan.

'If it comes to that, I don't like your tattoos,' says Ray Crooner. 'And the judge will almost certainly not like your tattoos What is that one on your forehead?'

'That's the Angel of Death,' says Cyan.

'Anyway, I don't think this …. Moon, what kind of name is that anyway ….. this *Moon* not liking your tattoos is going to get us far in terms of mitigation,' says Ray. 'The judge will take one look at those unsightly markings and your ….. barrage of nasal jewellery and make a decision influenced by this.'

'Haven't we got to go to magistrates first?' says Cyan.

'Yes, we do have to go to magistrates first,' says Ray. 'But really, do you think that magistrates are going are going to look favourably on someone who resembles a degenerate troglodyte. They probably won't even ask your name or give you the Bible to swear on. They pass cases like yours straight on. I might as well not turn up.'

'How about this then,' says Cyan. 'I went to a heavy metal festival where *Devil's Henchmen* force fed me a vicious cocktail of mind-bending drugs and dragged me off screaming to a tattoo marquee. It was like a descent into Hell. While *Dark Funeral* were playing, Satanic forces took over and before I knew it I was hearing voices in my head telling me to kill Moon.'

'Better,' says Ray. 'We might just be able to keep the sentence beneath twelve months.'

Jet and Indigo have recently returned from an ashram in Goa, where they have been receiving spiritual guidance from Swami Govinda and buying kaftans for Jet's new wardrobe. They have moved in together. Jet now gets up at five every morning, takes Bono for a quick walk and does a half an hour's Tai Chi, before his bowl of whole grain cereal with goji berries and manuka honey. He now has a healthy outdoor job working with wildlife. He practices yoga, in fact when Indigo is busy, he says he is going to run the class for her. They meditate to a CD with sounds of running water. Their new apartment is awash with aloe vera and weeping fig plants to purify the air. He works out at the gym and he takes a veritable orchestra of vitamins and supplements. He cycles everywhere, well nearly everywhere. When he does take the car, he listens to soothing music, Einaudi, Eno or Enya. He never drinks alcohol.

'Do you think we should visit Cyan in Holloway?' he says to Indigo, as he mixes the smoothies. It has been on his mind lately that she may not have had any visitors.

Indigo wants him to get back to massaging her thighs. 'Soon,' she says. 'Perhaps we will visit her soon.'

## Just The Way It Is

A second did not seem an important integer, but therein lay the problem. It was such a small unit of time. Yet, such was the degree of precision operating in the overcrowded skies that if Quincey Sargent had returned from his break seven seconds earlier or seven seconds later, the dreadful accident would not have happened. Sargent would not have given the instruction that resulted in the collision between the two leviathans that changed, albeit ever so slightly, Earth's path around the sun.

Had the accident not happened, things would be as they had always been. Earth would spin on its axis once every twenty four hours and revolve around the sun in its normal orbit every three hundred and sixty five days. There would still be thirty one million, five hundred and thirty six thousand seconds in a calendar year. But as you know there are now more. Just how many more has still to be calculated accurately. We hear new estimates every day with eminent scientists forever trying to steal a march on one another. No one can even say for sure that Earth's orbit is going to settle into a regular pattern. As you will be aware, the uncertainty has played havoc with digital technology and really messed up schedules and timetables. Try catching the eight o'clock Eurostar now.

Quincey Sargent has of course been dealt with, along with Stanton Kelso at ATC who failed to notice that the two giant craft were on a collision course. You probably saw Sargent and Kelso's execution on television, if you have one that still works. But knowing that they were punished can never make up for the hundreds of thousands of lives that were lost. I expect from time to time some of you still take a look at the film of the explosion on *topnet*, if you can get *topnet*, to remind yourselves.

But it is not only the measurement of time that we have to consider. The accident has a far greater legacy, affecting every area of our lives. We're only just beginning to find out the full extent of the disruption it has caused.

My friend, Ɑl, who works at the spy base calls me up out of the blue. He says that many of the strange phenomena that might be attributable to the catastrophe are being hushed up. Ɑl is not a

*WikiLeaks* scaremonger. When ᏀI tells me something I believe him. I trust ᏀI implicitly. We go back a long way. We belonged to the same motorcycle club, *The Diabolos* when we were younger. He rode a Triumph Bonneville and I had a Norton Commando. You build up trust when you are riding fast bikes on long runs in large groups like this. Margins of error are small. ᏀI would not lie to me now.

'I'm sure you've noticed that your satnav no longer works and there aren't nearly as many websites as there once were,' he says. '

'Of course,' I say. 'As you know digital is my field.'

'Quite! Time is well and truly screwed, isn't it?' he says. 'Anything that depends on time or needs a timer to operate, forget it.

'At least you no longer need to keep looking at your watch.' I say. 'Do you know? Even the oven timer is kaput and I've no idea when to put the cat out. In fact, the cat no longer wants to go out.'

'Who can blame it with all that fog?' he says. 'But, there's a whole bunch of other stuff that for whatever reason is not being reported. Why has an eight kilometre wide trench opened up across Central Asia?' he says. 'I don't think that has been on the news. Why are they keeping the lid on that?'

'Perhaps they have been too preoccupied with the floods in Nevada and Arizona to report on it,' I say.

'Why have the people in Australia started talking in a language that no one understands? Why do goats no longer have shadows.' he says. 'And what's happened to all the fish in the sea?'

'You think it's all part of a big cover-up then,' I say.

'The communication satellites weren't taken out by the explosion like they told us,' he says. 'They've been shut down since. And it's not our people that are doing it. There's definitely something sinister going on.'

I tell ᏀI about the after images that have begun to appear on all my photos. 'They make it look like people are slowly leaving or arriving,' I say. 'It is as if I have set a long exposure or superimposed a series of images on one another.'

ᏀI tells me that others are having the same problem. A friend of his finds he has a Serbian First World War ambulance superimposed on all his pictures and someone else he knows has a spectral German shepherd in every shot. Every day he says he comes across more and more curious things that cannot be explained.

'I'm wondering whether we are seeing more strange things lately, CI, because we're beginning to expect things to be odd,' I say. 'Aren't we looking for weirdness?'

'I suppose you might have a point, Bob,' he says. 'But I'm guessing that you don't really believe that what you say explains everything. There are just so many things that have changed. Life bears no resemblance to how it used to be. Look! There is one important thing that has never been revealed and no-one seems to have picked up on it. What was on board those two craft that collided? We just don't know. The Ministry hasn't been able to find out. Our allies haven't been able to find out. Nobody seems to know. Which is where you come in.'

'I do? You'll have to make that a little clearer,' I say.

'Well, Bob. For obvious reasons I can't go public with any of the information I come across. I mean, look what happened to Eddie Snowden. I don't want to have to live like that.'

'What you are saying is that I can, is that it?'

'Pretty much, Bob. I know that the internet is a bit skinnier than it once was, but you've got the skills to set up a proxy website and you know all there is to know about SEO, if that is the right expression and assuming that search engines still work. You could at least begin to post information for me. At the same time, you could discretely find out what other people might be noticing that we are not being told and report back.'

'But .....'

'You will get paid.'

'It's not that. It's .....'

'I know. I know. I work in the secrecy business. But there's a limit. When something this serious is going down, I don't think you should keep people in the dark. What do you say?'

I don't have anything better to do. I no longer have a job. Nobody seems to need digital display designers anymore. I suppose I could get a job repairing cars or something. With all the electrics failing that's where the demand is. But everyone's going to be turning their hand to that. I agree to CI's proposal.

I try to think of a suitable name for the site. aintthatthetruth.com, wtfshappening.com, alliwantisthetruth.com, none of them very snappy. Surprised that the domain hasn't been taken, I settle on whistleblower.com.

CI comes up with staggering tales from the word go, extraordinary stories from around the world. He wants people to know that they have started practising voodoo in Switzerland. He wants it out there that everybody in Japan has become left handed. That there are giant badgers in Nepal. The reason that the fish are all dead it is now thought is that there is no salt left in the sea. They have moved the International Date Line three times in a week and changed the value of pi. The latest on the length of a day is now that it is believed to be twenty five hours and twenty four minutes in old time. CI says that no-one is talking about the number of seconds in a year anymore. This he says is going to be impossible to calculate until Earth's orbit has settled.

My site begins to attract whistleblowers from around the world. *Rigatony* posts that Venice is sinking fast and that everyone in Padova is having identical disturbing dreams at night. Plastic has become unstable and computer keyboards and TV remote controls are decomposing, posts *MercyCaptain*. According to *Kommunique,* all the babies born in Kyrgyzstan since the catastrophe have been female, not a popular option in a Muslim country. There are dust storms in Oklahoma says *CrashSlayer*. Aren't there often dust storms in Oklahoma?

A lively online community quickly comes together through the forum. My admin duties keep me busy day and night. In no time at all the analogue hit counter is up to five figures. Although there's nothing directly relating to the cargoes of the craft, a majority of the posts are constructive and informative. Being an open forum there are of course also time wasters and religious fanatics. Fire and brimstone and Sodom and Gomorrah are mentioned a lot. What we are witnessing, the evangelists claim, is God's punishment for planned parenthood, spare parts surgery and gay marriage.

There have always been conspiracy theories, so it is unsurprising that some of these also find their way on to whistleblower.com pages. Everything going wrong it is claimed is part of a plan by ruthless aliens who want to force us into submission so they can take over

Earth. It is an Illuminati or Zionist plot to take over the planet. It is part of a big budget surreality television show. Everything is an illusion anyway. Some things you have to take with a pinch of salt. Nothing resembling a conclusive explanation for the upheaval appears, although the illusion explanation, while clearly impossible to confirm, is tempting. Everything that is happening might well be part of someone's dream. Or a hologram. Gravity in the universe comes from thin, vibrating strings. These strings are holograms of events that take place in a simpler, flatter cosmos. The holographic principle suggests that, like the security chip on your credit card, there is a two-dimensional surface that contains all the information needed to be able to describe a three-dimensional object, our universe. In essence, the information containing a description of a volume of space, be it a person or our Earth could be hidden in a region of this flattened *real* version of the universe.

It's a bit of a head-banger. I put this to ꃅ as best I can.

He agrees that multiverses and strings are legitimate lines of enquiry and the Ministry has been putting resources into their research. But how does this help?

'We have a whole heap of strangeness, that we didn't have before,' he says. 'If parallel worlds could explain what is happening, we would have had the kind of anomalies we are getting now all along. There would have always been parallel worlds. That's not what it is.'

It is difficult to disagree with him. Quantum mechanics even in its simpler form is something I have never been able to grasp, despite watching many programmes about it on television.

ꃅ goes on to tell me I am doing a good job and if I keep at it, all should be revealed. There is bound to be an explanation for the apparent rupture in the space-time continuum. So that's what it is, a rupture in the space-time continuum.

One moment I am sat at my computer, keying in a report about the dense swarm of black moths that has appeared over London, the next I am in a darkened room. The space is unfamiliar. It is small. There are no windows. There is a dank smell. The door is locked. I can hear the hollow sound of a slow but steady drip of water. I have always suffered from claustrophobia. Being confined like this has always been my deepest secret fear. I am terrified. This feels like the grave. Is this what death is like? Is this how it happens? Could this be it? No blinding light. No life flashing before your eyes. No white tunnel. Is this it? The other side? Or, perhaps it's the waiting chamber, the holding bay.

This is not it. Sometime later, it may be hours, minutes or even seconds, my captors reveal themselves. Not before I have been to hell and back. The door opens and they materialise slowly as if they are made up of dots, like a halftone in an old newspaper. There are three of them. As my eyes get used to the light I can see that they are three-dimensional figures and they are wearing military fatigues. They don't look friendly. There are no welcoming gestures. They have guns.

The one on the right of the group opens his mouth to speak. The sound appears to come from the one on the left, the one with the scar down his cheek and the alligator grin. 'You will close the website down,' he barks.

'Immediately,' says the one on the right. The sound appears to come from the one on the left. This one has a gallery of Japanese Dragon tattoos on his arms.

'We would have taken it down ourselves, but you did something ……. smart with it,' says the one in the centre. He is built like a Sherman tank and aptly he is the one with the biggest gun. It is pointing directly at my head.

Beneath my fear, I can't help thinking that this is a heavy-handed approach. Just one of them, any one of them could have knocked me up at home, pointed a gun at my head and expected to get results. You would not mistake these people for boy scouts. They really look like killers.

'We are the time police,' says Alligator Grin.' This may not be what he says, but this is how I hear it. Perhaps they are the time police. Perhaps they are not. Perhaps they are hallucinations but I am not taking that chance. My survival mechanism tells me that they are armed and I am not.

'We are here to set the record straight,' says Dragon Tattoos.

'To put an end to all that nonsense you've been publishing,' says Tank.

'Lies,' says Alligator Grin. At least I think that's what he says. His diction is not good.

18

'There's only one reality,' says Dragon Tattoos.

'And it's not yours,' says Tank.

'You are going to start again on your server and tell people the facts,' says Dragon Tattoos.

'The real facts,' says Tank. They have lost the rhythm. It's not his turn to speak.

'The day is twenty Ferraris,' says Alligator Grin. I'm getting the hang of it now. He means twenty four hours.

'And there are sixty minutes to the hour, and sixty seconds to the minute,' says Dragon Tattoos.

'The same as it has always been,' says Tank. For a moment, I think he is about to pull the trigger, but if he does that then the website is still going to be there.

'And the earth sorbet has always been the same,' says Alligator Grin. Perhaps he means Earth's orbit.

'You will say all the rest was a misapprehension.' I lose track of who is saying what. They are firing phrases at me like bullets. I feel dizzy. The room is spinning.

'A result of an over-active imagination,'

'Too much science fiction,'

'Choo many movies,'

'Too many video games,'

One moment I am face to face with three menacing mercenaries, the next moment I am back in front of my computer at home. The mercenaries must have been an hallucination caused by the stress of being in the darkened room. The darkened room might itself have been a delusion. It's hard to tell what is really happening anymore. But, here I am at home. I breathe a sigh of relief. But I'm not out of the woods yet. Two men in dark suits are with me in the room. One looks like a Mormon missionary, the other looks like Napoleon Solo. They both have guns. They are both pointed at me.

'You have not heard from Cl,' says Mormon missionary. This is a statement.

'You are not going to be seeing Cl,' says Napoleon Solo. This too is a statement.

'Cl died in a motorcycle accident in 1999.' Mormon Missionary again.

'So let's get started on the *new* website,' says Napoleon Solo. He is beginning to look less like Napoleon Solo. More Reservoir Dogs. Is it the way he angles his gun? Or is it the look of intent he has on his face? Mr Blue, perhaps.

'People need to know what's *really* going on,' says Mormon Missionary. He begins to look a little less like a Mormon missionary. More Men in Black.

'sameasiteverwas.com,' says Mr Blue.

'And put this little piece of …….. worm software on the back of it,' says Man In Black. 'It will take over all internet browsers and stop anyone getting access to any …….. rogue sites.'

'People will be able to sleep easy in their beds, with the assurance that everything is OK,' says Mr Blue.

'And know that someone is looking out for them,' says Man In Black. 'Like a big brother.'

I begin to see how it is that history is always written by the ones with the guns, the ones with the biggest guns, whoever they might be. The ones who can manipulate the media, whatever the media might be. How science at any point in time is what the scientists of the day tell us, however erroneous, and why God persists, albeit in one or two different versions. The people who are in charge make the rules, all the rules. They are the ones that dictate what is true and what is lies and that their way is the way it has always been. They establish their set of beliefs as facts and employ militia to enforce their truth, their version of events. They quash dissent. They find out what people's fears are and work on them until they are too frightened to disagree. There are no ways of seeing. There is just the one way, their way. Their version of events will always be the one that has always been. If necessary they will burn books and rewrite history. They will put worms onto your computer. They will destroy civilisations to make the oven timer work. You will know exactly when you have to put the cat out.

Earth will revolve around the sun in the same way at the same distance and there will always be thirty one million, five hundred and thirty six second in a year until such time as the people in charge say otherwise. Goats will always have shadows, Switzerland will never practice voodoo. Plastic will continue to be stable. Venice will not sink. There will always be fish in the sea. There will never be a multiverse.

Pi will always be three point one four one six. The same as it ever was. There will only be one reality. All the rest will be make believe. That's just the way it is.

# Kosmic Kitchen

## June 1970

Mark is eighteen years old and like many others of his generation is not sure what to do with his life. He has not given it any serious thought. Plans are for straights. Plans are not cool. Something will land in his lap when the time comes; when the world realises how talented he is. Perhaps he'll be a rock star, he imagines. He can sing Get Back just like Paul McCartney and on a good day play John's guitar solo note for note. And he has written four of his own songs.

Mark is sitting; perhaps sprawling might be a better description, on a pile of paisley cushions in a room painted in psychedelic patterns. Although it is hot outside the windows are closed and a haze of blue smoke hangs in the air. As soon as a joint gets near its end, one or other of Mark's loose group of companions rolls another. People might drift in and drift out without ceremony, but while they are here, this is an unspoken house rule. Mark has only recently boarded the metaphorical starship, and is still a little disorientated by space, but the feeling of strangeness seems to him an altogether pleasant one.

*Ummagumma* is playing. *Ummagumma* is one of three LPs that are played in random rotation, along with *Hot Rats* and *Trout Mask Replica*. *Ummagumma* and *Trout Mask Replica* are double albums so perhaps that should be five. None are ever returned to their sleeves. Sometimes *Electric Ladyland* takes a turn or *The White Album*, although this is badly scratched on side two and sticks on *Bungalow Bill*. 'What did you kill, what did you kill,' ad infinitum. *Led Zeppelin 2* completes the record collection but this does not leave its sleeve. *Led Zeppelin* are too popular and therefore, uncool. The cover, therefore, is just used for rolling joints on. *Gold Leb* is around at the moment, but Mark has a piece of *Nepalese black*, which he is saving for later.

*Ummagumma* is the best one for astral travelling, Mark thinks, especially *Astronomy Domine*. Pink Floyd are his favourite band. In between conversations with his fellow conspirators about mystic discovery, thought control and the brain police, Mark has the hots for Vashka. Vashka is about five feet ten and has recently arrived from the coast, or was it the moon. Short-term memory loss is a frequent problem. She came through the door, or was it the bathroom window, with a denim tote bag, an acoustic guitar, and a kite and said, 'Hi. I'm Vashka. I've come to stay.' She has taken her jeans off now to be more comfortable and is sitting in her pants but no one seems to have taken much notice, except Mark. She is a Sagittarius.

The cottage, which they are squatting, is called Kosmic Kitchen and is painted in bright colours outside, mostly orange and yellow, to attract visitors from outer space to this quiet corner of the middle of nowhere. Quasar comes from outer space, they suspect. Quasar arrived yesterday or maybe it was last week. (time disorientation is a frequent problem) in a jet-black left hand drive VW camper with runic symbols stencilled on the sides and is now asleep on a rug upstairs, dreaming perhaps about black holes and quarks. There is no proper furniture in Kosmic Kitchen, just one or two saggy mattresses and an assortment of mismatched cushions and rugs. As sleep is a last resort here on the frontiers of time and space, Quasar must have come a long way.

## June 1994

Nuala is driving to see a client in her GTE. She is listening to *Nevermind*. She likes Nirvana because Kurt Cobain killed himself with a gun. 'I swear that I don't have a gun,' he is singing. The song is *Come As You Are*, recorded four years before he shot himself. Nuala is thirty four but on the phone, she says she is twenty eight. She is five feet ten but does not draw attention to her height. She is a dress size too big, through habitual overindulgence, but on the phone describes herself as nicely curved and calls herself Venus. She is Venus now in her short skirt and black stockings as she drives too fast down country lanes towards the place with the unpronounceable name. She describes her periodic amphetamine weight management programme as *seeing Billy*. She has seen Billy twice today. The GTE has a digital display speedo and she amuses herself by watching the orange numbers soar as she puts her foot down.

Her mobile phone rings. It is John from the agency. She does not know who John is and John does not know who she is. They have, as far as she is aware, never met. John phones her up at her home to let her know the numbers of prospective clients. She then calls them to arrange a time and place and after she has done the business she sends banknotes in an envelope to a PO Box. John is phoning her now on her mobile to tell her that the number the caller gave for this job does not check out with the information on his database. He says he has been trying to call her for ages, but it seems there is poor coverage in this quiet corner of the middle of nowhere.

Venus is apprehensive now. She does not know whether to go on or turn back. Some of the people in small Welsh villages have unusual sexual preferences. But, of course, there is the money. And what's the worst that can happen? A few bruises maybe. 'I love myself better than you,' sings Kurt Cobain. The song is *On a Plain*. This is Nuala's favourite. She turns it up and drives on, faster now.

## June 1970

Mark gets up and turns the record over. His mouth is dry. No one ever makes tea or coffee in Kosmic Kitchen. Perhaps there is none. Or if there is, there is almost certainly no milk or sugar. He is hungry. He is sure that there is nothing in the kitchen, other than some sunflower seeds, some shrivelled carrots and a bag of flour. He has a vague recollection that he checked the kitchen for comestibles earlier, or maybe it was yesterday. Nourishment does not the prime concern for the seasoned space traveller. The last time someone cooked was he thinks when Rollo made the acid pie, with a batch of the *purple haze*. This Mark reckons was three days ago. It certainly rocked the starship. The whole universe seemed to be melting at one point.

No one in the house has done any shopping for as long as he can remember, other than the occasional run to the garage for pasties and crisps in John's A30 van. The nearest shop is four miles away, and John went off somewhere yesterday in the A30 van with Rabbit. And of course, Quasar is upstairs asleep, dreaming of matter and antimatter. Mark hopes someone will arrive soon with some chocolate. All things must pass and people do have the habit of dropping in unexpectedly in this haphazard corner of the cosmos.

'Go with the flow,' Maggot keeps telling him. 'Light is light and shadow is shadow, like yin and yang. When you're meant to go up, go up to the highest point and when you're meant to go down, go down to the lowest point. Sometimes there is no flow. If there is no flow, then be still and wait for the flow to begin again. But never resist the flow.'

Maggot along with Maggie was one of the first to arrive at Kosmic Kitchen. They had considered calling it Maggie's Farm, even Maggot's Farm, but someone, perhaps it was Rockit, came up with the Kosmic Kitchen and the name just stuck. Mark sits down again, next to Vashka now. Marvin, who recently arrived from California, or was it Andromeda, hands him a fat spliff. Mark takes a greedy pull on it and feels revived. *As Set the Controls For the Heart of the Sun* swirls around his consciousness he has visions of Venus and orange skies.

## June 1994

As the GTE powers its way through the Welsh hills, Nuala reflects on the time before she did all this running around the country. The ennui of daily repetition as she sat at home raising children and watching *Pebble Mill, Neighbours,* repeats of *Dallas* and mindless children's programmes while Roy was out fixing boilers to bring home the bacon. Before the fire and before Holly and Polly were taken into care.

She remembers too, endlessly taking advantage of Roy's naivety and trust. When early on in their relationship she had told Roy that she had a deep dark secret, he had said that it didn't matter. So she had never told him about it. As she changes down into third to overtake a procession of slower cars, she remembers Roy accepting that she needed a break from twinkling little stars and the wheels on the bus going round and round. And that she liked to go out in the evenings, leaving him to clear up and put her girls to bed. And leaving him to do all the housework at weekends, while she went to the hairdressers or shopping on the High Street for shoes she never wore. And he did not seem to mind that she frequently came home noisily in the early hours. He may even have realised that she had a string of lovers. Surely it must have been obvious that she did not go out dressed like she did to go to evening classes or girly chats over a bottle of Liebfraumilch. And the messages men left for her on the answerphone must have hinted at her infidelity. Not that he ever complained on the occasions she woke him in the middle of the night to give her a good *seeing to*. What she is doing now she feels is not so very different from what she has always done, except that now she gets paid for doing it. And she loves the roar of the engine and the squeal of brakes as she negotiates a blind bend in the middle of the road and narrowly misses a cattle truck.

# June 1984

Mark is sitting in a coffee shop in Amsterdam with his friend, John. They are a little drunk and a little stoned. A blues band is playing *Third Stone from the Sun*, an old Jimi Hendrix song. Mark has just had an argument with his girlfriend, Sasha. She has stormed off, and John's girlfriend, Laura has gone after her. The four of them have come to Amsterdam for a stress-free break from their nine to five jobs. After the initial regret about their argument, Mark feels relieved that Sasha has gone. Something was in the air between them all day. Nothing that he said or did met with her approval. Perhaps Sasha is premenstrual, he thinks. Why else would she get upset about the magazines that he had bought, or that he had suggested they take in a strip show instead of an Indonesian restaurant. They will make up later, he expects.

He apologises to John and orders two more pilsners for the two of them, and John lights a spliff to cool things down. They talk about Piet Mondrian, avant-garde cinema and Dutch taxi drivers. Mark has his eye now on a statuesque beauty with long dark hair who is standing with another girl at the other end of the bar. She is dressed in black and must be about five foot ten, he thinks, and she is wearing high heels. He remarks to John that the girl, who he is convinced is also giving him the eye, reminds him of Vashka. John agrees that she does at this moment in time present a tempting alternative to Sasha, but says that he never met Vashka. Mark tries to jog his memory, reminding him of the crazy days all those years ago at Kosmic Kitchen. John suggests that perhaps Vashka may have arrived after he had gone off with Rabbit to work on the oil rigs. Whatever happened to Rabbit? they wonder. Or Flipper? Or Jesus? And what about Dave and Dave Too? Do you remember when they used to sell acid along with hamburgers from the hot dog van? John asks. And what about Quasar? With his monologues about quantum theory. And ley lines. And orgone energy. Quasar was, they agree, a nutcase.

The band starts to play a slow traditional twelve bar blues. John expresses the need to relieve himself and goes off in search of the toilet. The girl dressed in black comes over flicking her hair back seductively as she does so. She produces a thin neatly rolled spliff from her handbag and asks Mark for a light. He swallows nervously and digs deep into his pocket for his lighter. She introduces herself.

Her name she says is Nuala. Mark notices that she does not have a drink. They strike up a conversation about cocktails and he orders her a tequila sunrise. She says that she and her friend come to Amsterdam four or five times a year and that there is no place like it for getting your rocks off. She rubs her hand slowly down her thigh to communicate to Mark what she means. Mark tells her it is his first visit. Having said it, he feels at a disadvantage and a little apprehensive. He is more accustomed to being in control of the situation. He is not sure how to react with someone so forward. He looks round for John, who has not reappeared. The bar has suddenly become more crowded. A poster advertising Galaxy Coffee Shop catches Mark's attention.

'What star sign are you,' he asks, out of desperation for something to say.

'Sagittarius with Leo rising,' she says. 'And my moon is in Sagittarius too.'

'A lot of fire there for someone who doesn't have a lighter,' remarks Mark.

Nuala does not seem to wish to pursue the astrological theme. Instead, out of the blue, she says, 'I expect you'd like to come back to my room and fuck me .'

Mark is taken aback and wonders perhaps if she might be a prostitute, but does not want to ask. Sensing his concern, Nuala quickly clears up the misunderstanding, and giving Mark little chance to decline the offer leads him away by the hand.

## June 1988

Quasar is living on the island of Lanzarote in an imposing villa built out of black volcanic stone. To maximise its darkness, the doors and window frames are painted matt black, and the windows themselves are tinted. It is perhaps the largest house in the village and it blends in perfectly with the volcanic ash in which it is set, but stands out dramatically when viewed against the other buildings nearby, which are uniformly painted white. It is surrounded by a collection of arcane sculptures in various stages of completion. The largest of the sculptures, dominating the lunar landscape appears to be a model of the solar system. Some of the other pieces too seem to represent stellar objects. Another according to its plaque depicts the angel of death, and on the black tiled patio, there is a sinister study of a twisted human skeleton. There are also sculptures of erotically entwined limbs scattered at random amongst tenebrous towering cacti. The sculptures all have one thing in common; they are jet black. A tall radio mast stands in the grounds of the house and there is an immense satellite dish on the roof between the solar panels and the water storage tanks. An astronomical telescope is positioned to catch the light from the stars of the southern sky. The island is reputedly one of the best places in the world for stargazers to view the cosmos.

Quasar keeps himself to himself. To add to the mystique, he wears Arab dress and makes no attempt to learn to speak Spanish. If anyone speaks to him in English too he pretends not to understand. Given the potential for communication he has with other worlds, perhaps he doesn't feel the need for social intercourse. He works in an underground studio where he plays reverberating electronic music that sounds as if it is coming from the bowels of the earth or perhaps the outer reaches of the Milky Way.

It is Thursday. A red Renault draws up outside Quasar's gate and a Sylvia Krystel look-alike in a short red dress steps out. She looks conspicuous in this achromatic setting. Dogs bark and an old man outside the historic black and white church down the road makes the sign of the cross. Sylvia is about five feet ten and is wearing heels. A stiff breeze coming in from the Sahara lifts her dress as she makes her way across the picon. The front door opens and she disappears inside. She will stay for three hours, as she does every Monday and Thursday. The old man crosses himself once more. Set in tradition the people in the village understandably disapprove of Quasar. They view all of his activities with equal proportions of suspicion and fear. Rumours have circulated among them that he is a Satanist or worse, the devil. Some even believe he is a cannibal. Shortly, following the disappearance of a girl from a neighbouring village, the strength of bad feeling towards him will see him deported from the island.

## June 2006

Leo is twenty one. He is sitting at his desktop computer eating a poppy bagel and a kabano sausage. He has a bag of *Doritos*, a selection of dips that he bought earlier at Morrisons, and a glass of Belgian cider. He is catching up on the emails in his inbox. He has about two dozen, about half of which are introducing him to new mobile phone offers with hundreds of free minutes and free texts, or trying to sell him penis enlargements or Viagra. Does everyone receive these? he wonders. Others suggest ways to make his business more profitable. What business? Or try to sell him cheap software. All his software is unregistered, anyway. He does not need Guaranteed Cheapest Prices on *Office 2007*, *Adobe CS3*, or *Quark*. And he has never heard of *Quasar*. Perhaps it is a new web browser. He sets about deleting the mail, pausing briefly to read one or two messages that he thinks might be of interest.

Leo has been trying to trace his parents for several months now since he became aware that he had been adopted. He discovered that Dave Too and Vashka were not his real parents when he came home from university for the winter break to find the house empty and the Crosby Nash estate agents board outside. 'Under Offer,' it said. He phoned his paternal grandfather in Swindon, who had been glad to have someone to talk to about the slugs on his allotment and the new road they were building outside his house, despite protests from all the residents in his street and a letter to the Deputy Prime Minister. After a chat about his arthritis and the lamentable state of the NHS, Leo had managed to get a number that he could phone his *father* on.

'I think there's been a bit of a rift, young Leo,' Grandfather Too had told him. 'Tread carefully.'

He caught up with his father, drowning his sorrows in a pub called *The Black Hole*. Over a pint and chaser, followed by a chaser and chaser, Dave Too told him that he and Vashka had separated, but that it didn't matter because he was not their son anyway. They had he said been meaning to tell him for years, but there was never seemed to be a right time to break the news. From the angry exchanges that ensued and a bitter reunion with a tearful Vashka later the same day in *The Blind Monkey*, Leo was only able to deduce that their breakup may have had something to do with an unexpected visit from Dave (One). With oceans of alcohol by now washing through his brain, he was unable to establish exactly what the connection was, or what had happened, or who was to blame. He left with the profound feeling of betrayal and abandonment, and the conclusion that both 'parents' were selfish and remorseless. The cold light of day only served to strengthen his feeling of detachment and he has had no contact with either of them                                                                                             since.

Since returning to university, where he is reading Creative Writing, Leo has spent dozens of hours trawling through internet websites, following links to ever more unconventional source material and has discovered that his real mother may have been called Nuala Du Maurier. And that she may have died in 1994 when she disappeared in mysterious circumstances in Wales. An Astra GTE registered in her name was found abandoned in a local beauty spot, but investigations into her disappearance which briefly occupied the divisional police force were able to draw no conclusions, and the case was closed. His own efforts tracing her have drawn a blank. There has been no record of her since 1994. None of the people he has managed to track down that knew her have been able to shed any light on the circumstances of her disappearance, although one or two did mention someone called John that she was in contact with. John, of course, is a fairly common name.

Leo pours another glass of Belgian cider and picks up a half smoked joint from the ashtray and lights it. The television is on in the background. It is the World Cup. England are playing Sweden, but Leo is not really paying much attention. It will probably be a nil-nil draw, he thinks. It often is in these big games where there are high expectations. He shares a house with three other students, but they are in the Union bar. It is nearly the end of term and they are all getting ready to go home for the summer. Leo, having no family home to go back to, thinks he may stay on for a few more weeks.

Leo has also had little success in tracing his real father, the only clue to his identity coming from a newspaper report in the archives of the North Devon Gazette and Advertiser, dated September 1984, about a Mark Friday and a Nuala du Maurier winning a karaoke competition in Ilfracombe sponsored by Venus Fashions singing *It Takes Two*. Given that he was born in April 1985, this would have been the early months of his mother's pregnancy. The fact that Nuala and Mark were at the seaside together, in a particularly low-key resort, suggests to Leo that they must have been very close and that Mark Friday might, therefore, be his father.

Despite Friday being an uncommon surname, all his investigations have produced no trace of Mark. The closest match is a Mike Friday who is 86 and living in a nursing home in Lyme Regis. The email with the subject *Man Friday* that has just arrived in his inbox and he is about to open could be of significance, he thinks. It has an attachment. What Leo does not know is that the attachment contains a virus that will cripple his computer and with it destroy the intricate murder mystery he has been writing about a latter-day hippy and a femme fatale.

Without his computer, it may also take Leo a little while to see that Mark and John have become Facebook friends. The computers at the university will not allow you to log in to Facebook.

Had he been able to he would have seen that Mark would be listing his place of residence as Mundesley, North Norfolk. Not a large place.

# Stranger on the Shore

He was there lurking in the shadows each time we went to the beach. My dog, Tarquin, a salt and pepper schnauzer would sometimes bark agitatedly as we approached. Tarquin had a habit of running up to strangers to introduce himself, so I would at this point throw a stick for him to chase after, and avert my gaze. Something about this spectral figure suggested that that he wanted to be alone and I was intruding on his space. At first, I found his baleful presence intimidating but by and by I convinced myself there must be an innocent explanation for his being there alone every evening on this remote stretch of the coast. Perhaps he was camping there. People had been known to camp on the beaches around here in the summer – at least until they were moved on.

My argument was that if he were a fugitive from justice or a child molester, he would surely have been caught by now. Besides, if he were the latter, this would not be the place to come. Very few children ventured on to this rough shingle. There were much better beaches for children a few miles away. This was a dog beach. And certainly not the most accessible dog beach. Perhaps he was an erstwhile mariner or a solitary poet or something. Whichever, it was clear that he did not want to make contact with me in any way. He was so well camouflaged that at first you might not notice he was there at all. He seemed to have the ability to find shadow where there was none and like a chameleon blended in perfectly with his surroundings so that at a distance of say ten or twenty yards, he was of indeterminate age or race. Tarquin and I gradually became accustomed to his clandestine behaviour. It became just a normal feature of our evening walks. After a week or two Tarquin did not even bother to bark at him.

Had I found him particularly disturbing I could have easily taken Tarquin up the other side of the cove towards the cliff path for his walks, but since my retirement, I had to admit I had become a creature of habit. In fact, if I'm honest, I liked to walk this way because Amy and I used to come here when we were courting. The Spring of 1961, it would have been when we met. Spurs were top of the league (I could still name the whole first team) and *Wooden Heart* was at number one in the pop charts. Amy was a member of the Elvis Presley fan club. I took her to see *Flaming Star* at the Gaumont, or was it *Blue Hawaii*? I was more of a Cliff fan myself. Livin' Doll and Travelling Light. They were great tunes. Anyway, one time when I had my short back and sides at Reg Cropper's, I had gotten 'something for the weekend' and we fumbled about behind a clump of rocks. Yuri Gagarin was in space at the time I remember. Ever since then I've felt an attachment to this beach. Amy, bless her heart, died three years ago from complications after a routine operation. I was inconsolable. That's when I got Tarquin to keep me company, what with the children grown up and long gone. But I always thought of Amy when I walked this way.

I dropped news of my sightings casually into my daily conversations around the village. Mrs Chegwidden in the Post Office said she often went to the beach with her pastels, but had never seen him, nor had Spike at the garage where I had the Daewoo serviced. Barbara from the Age Concern Shop, who knew everything that went on around the area, hadn't heard anything. My neighbours Breok and Merryn had not seen him, and my other neighbours Jack and Vera suffered from an intermittent deafness and did not understand what I was saying. Mushtaq in the general store where I bought Tarquin's *James Wellbeloved* said he hadn't got time to go to the beach since Nasim had gone off to work at *The Eden Project*. No one seemed to have caught sight of my man of mystery but me. I wondered if P. C. Trescothick might know something, but after the incident with Tarquin and the sheep, I did not like to draw attention to myself.

I kept an eye on the local newspaper, in fact went to the library in the nearby town to look at back copies. I remembered the days when I used to take Adam and Alice there after work on a Monday when the library was open late to give Amy a bit of a break. We did this I recall for several years in our Kermit green *Deux Cheveaux*. I would take the opportunity look at the local paper while they were choosing their Roald Dahl or Stig of the Dump. There never seemed much to report in those days. It was a quiet backwater.

*The Advertiser* today described a different world. A serial killer who had preyed on female cab drivers in the locality had been apprehended. A man had died in a charity cliff plunge to raise money for Disabled Surfers. There was controversy over a proposed Dial a Drink scheme being introduced where alcohol could be delivered to your door 24 hours a day, this on top of the more liberal licensing laws that were leading to lawlessness after hours in the local market towns. There were reports of chilling attacks on pensioners outside the post office, and a piece about nightclubs and bars being issued with 'cocaine torches', that door staff could shine into clubbers faces, which would make microscopic particles of the drug glow green. Clubbers; the only club there used to be around here was the United Services Club. There was a story about a dancing goat that you could hire for parties and another about a woman who crashed her car while teaching her dog to drive. There were, however, no reports of a furtive interloper living on a shingle beach in my neck of the woods.

It was outside the library that I bumped into Mikey.

'Well Fuck me on a Friday, Frank! Good to see you, mate. It must be five years,' he said. He was tilting a little. I imagined he was no longer on the wagon.

I agreed it had been a long time. In fact, I hadn't seen Mikey since Amy's funeral.

He quickly confirmed my suspicions about the drinking.

'I'll tell you what old mate. Come and have a beer with Stan and me later. We've started going to The Buccaneer.'

'The Buccaneer?' I questioned. 'You can't be serious.'

The Buccaneer as I remembered it was a bit select. Amy and I had had our silver wedding celebration there. Silver Service. Thirty pound a head back then. Adam was going through his punk phase at the time and had come in his bondage gear with his orange hair and full regalia of safety pins, embarrassing us all. It would have been hard at the time to predict that he would become a science teacher in Cumbria. Pillar of the community, married with the standard two children and a Ford Focus. Alice's career path had been a tad unusual. After passing a City and Guilds Level 3 in the unlikely subject of Advanced Dog Grooming, she had opened a Dog Spa in the Cotswolds with her friend Terry. Terry, I should add is female. Probably no grandchildren there. My main regret I suppose was with the family so far flung, the only time I saw them was at Christmas. It could get lonely with just your own company all day long. There was Tarquin of course, but he was not a great conversationalist. Alice suggested I joined a dating agency but I wonder if I'm not a bit long in the tooth for all of that. Mikey's voice brought me out of my reverie.

'All the other pubs round here have been turned in bistros, Frankie, you know, posh nosh for the grockles,' he said.

'But the Buccaneer is the most exclusive of all the places around here.' I protested, looking him up and down. 'Surely they wouldn't let you in in your tatters.'

'You don't get out a lot, Frank, do you? The Bucc went into a downward spiral in the nineties,' he said. 'Fortune Inns you might remember went bust. It was empty for yonks, five years or more. If you don't count the hippy squatters. No one wanted it. Till The Flynns took it. Doesn't do food anymore, well you can get scotch eggs and crisps. Cheapest beer around here, though...... All the holiday people go to The Yacht or The Jolly Slaver for their t-bone steaks or salmon in white wine sauce.'

'Whole new world round here, Mikey, Seems determined to leave us the likes of me behind,' I said. 'Do you know what? Remember Rose Trevillick? I've just read in the paper that she has been fined for feeding the ducks in the park. What is going on?'

Mikey did not remember Rose. Or the park.

'Stan's doing well,' he said. 'He'll be really pleased to see you. 'Keeps talking about the time the two of you took the boat out around the headland that really bad winter.'

I had known Stan and Mikey for over twenty years. The three of us had worked together for a time doing shifts at the china clay factory. 'Worked' of course might have been a euphemism in Mikey's case. He spent most of the time at the factory avoiding it. When you first met Mikey, you would listen to his stories with rapt attention. He had been junior billiards champion of the South West. He had had a trial for Plymouth Argyle Football Club. He had been the fifteenth person to complete the Rubik Cube. He had once been a roadie with Cream, and claimed to have once had a fling with Christine Perfect, or was it Julie Driscoll. To look at Mikey, all eighteen stone of him and not an inch over five feet four, you would have to say that either seemed unlikely. Stan, on the other hand, was someone on whose word you could rely. If Stan said that the Martians had landed you would expect to see little green men on your way to the Co-op. The thing was that Stan was quite likely to say that the Martians had landed. He had been for as long as I could remember into the study of UFOs. You might say Stan was impressionable but he was genuine.

The smoking ban meant we had to sit outside The Buccaneer, but as it was a nice evening I settled Tarquin down with a pork pie and a bowl of Guinness, and Mikey, Stan and I began to catch up. Mikey told me that he was back in the music business managing a Kinks tribute band called *The Kunts* – with a K. They had not as yet had many bookings but Mikey said they were good musicians and the singer looked just like Ray Davies circa 1966. 'Only a question of time before they make it,' he added.

'You don't think maybe the name might be the problem,' I said. 'I mean the punk era was 30 years ago.'

'Not at all mate,' said Mikey, There are bands called *The FuckFucks*, *The Smackheads*, *The Leper Coons*, *Alien Autopsy*, *Jesus Chrysler*, all sorts of irreverent names.'

'I shouldn't think many of them are on the tribute band circuit,' I said. 'There's a kind of respectability involved when you book a band at the local town hall.'

Mikey said he had not had a proper job since he was laid off from the china clay factory. He got by by signing on at two different addresses, doing cash in hand felt roofing, and selling pirate DVDs at car boots. I recollected Jack at the butchers telling me he had bought *Kill Bill* and *Inglorious Bastards* at a car boot and that he hadn't been able to play them on his machine. Mikey was so indiscreet. He spent the next ten minutes reeling off a catalogue of scams that he had been engaged in. Nothing big or dramatic, but every one it seemed at the expense of some poor unsuspecting victim. He had no morals. No wonder Irene had divorced him.

Mikey's mobile rang - *Smoke on the Water* by Deep Purple, giving Stan the opportunity to talk about his newly discovered fascination with 'rods'. I must have looked a little bewildered so he started at the beginning.

'Rods,' Stan explained 'are possibly the best evidence we have of alien life to date, These things move much too quickly to be seen with the naked eye, but they can be captured on film and seen when the film is played back in slow motion. They appear to have appendages along their torsos which move in a wave like motion, and the torsos bend as they move. Rods can be from a few inches to several feet in length. They have been filmed all over the world. I've started filming them.'

He showed me some of the still photos of 'rods' he carried around with him.

'Impressive, huh,' he said with a self-congratulatory smile. 'We could go filming one night down on that beach where you walk your dog, Frank. Round towards the cave. I'm sure we'd find there were rods there. What do you say?'

I was unconvinced. All the same, I agreed to go with him the following evening to look for rods. I had not had chance to bring the subject of the stranger on the shore into our conversation. I thought it would be better now not to mention it. This way I could just see what Stan made of him first hand. Mikey said he would not be able to make it.

'Sorry guys,' he said, grinning. 'I've got a date.'

Not being used to drinking so much *Old Thumper* I had just about recovered and taken Tarquin for a quick walk along the river bank when Stan picked me up late in the afternoon the following day. We both blamed the excess on Mikey and agreed that he had always been a bad influence.

'He's always been that way,' Stan said. 'Difficult to have just a pint or two when Mikey's around.'

'Not going to change now,' I agreed. 'What's this band he was talking about?'

'There is no band,' said Stan. 'He was just winding you up.'

'What about the date then,' I said'

'What do you think?' said Stan.

'Another Christine Perfect?'

'Or Julie Driscoll.'

'Lives in a fantasy world, doesn't he'

'Always has, always will.'

'Swift half?'

'Why not.'

We stopped off at The Buccaneer. It was nearly empty. Errol, the landlord explained to us how he had bought the place for a song, put on tap a good selection of strong ales and farmers' cider and within a few weeks business was booming, but lately, The Bucc' was going down the pan. He blamed the smoking ban. Most of his drinkers he said were also smokers. Also, a number of his guest beers had been *banned from sale* because they were too strong.

'And of course, there's the recession.' he said. 'Mikey's probably my only regular customer. And he's out on a date tonight he tells me.'

'Not going to bring her in here then,' added Stan.

'No I don't believe he will,' said Errol.

It was nearly twilight when we arrived at the beach, the ideal time, Stan said, to film rods. He had some sophisticated video equipment. Nikon. We unloaded it from his Land Rover and carried it along the deserted shingle. A flock of herring gulls began circling a little way off. Their distinct trumpeting echoed around the bay. I had read somewhere that you could detect eleven distinct calls, each with a different message. A stiff breeze was coming in off the sea so it took Stan took a minute or two to steady the tripod in the ground. He then carefully set the camera up.

'The secret is to use the sports setting,' he said. 'This will ensure you have a high shutter setting so each frame of video will look like a single picture without blur.'

I took his word for it. Maybe it had infra-red for night vision or some kind of thermal imaging. I was a bit of a technophobe so I did not like to ask. I was more interested to see whether he had noticed the shadowy figure in the scrub crouching behind the a clump of broom. It seemed he hadn't. I wondered whether I should prompt him. I left it awhile, during which time he continued to make tiny adjustments to the camera settings. He talked excitedly about someone called Jose Escamilla from New Mexico, who had been the first person to film rods.

'Over forty eight million people have visited his website and thousands have submitted photos of rods.' he said. 'I've put several of mine on the site. Jose emailed me to say how impressed he was by them.'

All the time he was speaking the figure did not move. He carried on crouching behind the scrub, camouflaged increasingly well by the gathering dusk. Stan peered through the viewfinder even though he had said that rods could not be seen with the naked eye, they only became visible during playback.

'Stan,' I said finally. 'What do you make of that fellow there hiding behind the rock?'

'Where? he said.

I pointed and he took a good look in that direction. He squinted myopically.

'I can't see anyone, Frank' he said.

'There,' I shouted, pointing again. The figure was indistinct now. He had blended in with the landscape. A few seconds later I could not see him at all. He had disappeared.

Stan hadn't at any stage picked up on the urgency of my quest and suggested that we moved on round to the cave before it became too dark. Stan had calculated also that there would be a window of a couple of hours before the tide was fully in. If we left it any longer we might find ourselves cut off. He handed me some equipment, folded up the tripod and off we set off into the gloaming. I was glad that I had not brought Tarquin. He did not like the cave very much. Perhaps it had something to do with the unusual acoustics.

Stan set up some backlighting and we spent an hour or so filming in the cave.

'I am sure rods are extraterrestrial.' he said. 'We are used to seeing aliens being portrayed as two legged, two armed, two eyed human-like beings. But the truth of the matter is, and again this is only my opinion, alien life should be, well.... alien! Rods demonstrate they have some type of intelligence, as they will often dodge things that they would otherwise collide with. I'll show you some of the film I've got later.'

While Stan held forth about the properties of rods and the incredible speeds they travelled at, I found myself looking for signs of the stranger, a sleeping bag or a backpack or something. The cave contained a random sample of the kind of marine litter one might expect to have been washed up and a few discarded food wrappers and crumpled beer cans, there was nothing suggest that anyone had been sleeping there recently.

On the way back I kept my eyes peeled for another glimpse and scanned the rocks with Stan's powerful torch, but he seemed to have gone into hiding. I took Tarquin down to the beach regularly over the next few days but not once did I catch sight of the outlander. I looked amongst the scrub and sat for hours on a rock listening to the surf wash up on the shingle in the hope that he might suddenly appear. There was no sign. I began to question whether I had ever seen him. After all, no one else had. Had I become obsessed by an apparition? Or had I stepped into the twilight zone?

I thought about what Stan had been saying about rods. About alien life being alien. There was so much we did not understand. I had for instance read a little about superstring theory. I had got bogged down in the detail, but the theory posits that all physical matter is made up of vibrating elements called 'strings' rather than ball-like particles of conventional physics. String theory proposes that there are eleven dimensions; four correspond to the three ordinary spatial dimensions and time while the rest are curled up and not perceptible. This would help to explain a number of things. In such a scheme of things why shouldn't there be rods? For that matter why shouldn't there be a presence on the beach that only I had been able to see? If you thought enough about them, most things were plausible. Like the idea of the expanding universe, it was best not to think too much about them.

I had made the decision to give up on my preoccupation with the stranger, when I got a call from Stan. He said that he had transferred the film he had taken at the beach onto to his computer and was going through it frame by frame. He wanted me to come over right away and have a look.

Fifteen minutes later Stan was ushering me into what he referred to as his editing suite. Scattered around the walls were a series of prints of what appeared to be oversized illuminated insects. I took these to be Stan's photos of rods. He sat me down in front of a Mac Pro with a large widescreen monitor. He then called up the media player clicked on a file and a film showing fairly unspectacular scenes of shingle and brush began playing. I watched as the camera panned along a small stretch of rocky outcrop. I recognised it of course, but it made dull viewing. Perhaps I was missing something. I had expected that he was going to show me some shots of rods from our visit to the cave.

'But have a look at this,' he said excitedly.

He stopped the film and played it from the beginning, jogging it forward one frame at a time. The images were a little hazy, but if you looked carefully, there was a figure crouched behind the rock just as I had seen him that night with Stan. Each frame confirmed his familiar presence.

'What do you think, Frank,' said Stan looking me in the eye. 'It's you, isn't it?'

We had stepped into the twilight zone. Sometimes the truth is stranger than fiction.

# Slumpton

The door to number 16 slammed in Harry's face, as it had more times than Harry cared to remember. Its split green and orange panels were all too familiar. Familiar too were the plywood and chicken wire that were nailed over the space where the window should have been, perhaps in a bygone age where a window once was. The force of the sudden closure caused a liberal sprinkling of masonry to dislodge itself from an upstairs window, landing on the shoulder of Harry's paint-smeared donkey jacket, where it did not look out of place. Even so, Harry brushed it off with the palm of his hand, and moved on down the street, past two boarded up terraced houses and a pile of rubble where others had until recently been, before arriving outside number 28. Sounds consistent with marital discord could be heard from within. Harry shuddered. He felt a strong urge to go back home. He was too old for this kind of aggravation. He lit a *Woodbine* and struggled to regain his composure. He must be resolute, he told himself. After all, the Luker family had been slum landlords since the thirties and this was 1980. His grandfather, George Luker had collected from these very houses during 'the blitz.' What would George have thought if he knew Harry was such a wuss?

His composure restored, Harry rapped firmly on the front door with his knuckles. This had the effect of bringing a corpulent, unshaven hulk of about forty face to face with him across the threshold. This was Natt, or 'Nasty' as he was known locally. There were signs of either a recent breakfast or perhaps last night's vomit, on the front of Nasty's vest - which was, in fact, the back, Harry observed, the garment being both back to front and inside out. Nasty towered above Harry and looked far from pleased at having been disturbed.

'M'morning N'nasty,' stammered Harry. 'Nice day again.'

'Pishoff,' snarled Nasty. He was not wearing his false teeth.

Wasting no further energy on social pleasantries with unwanted visitors, Nasty returned to the arena of family strife. Harry wiped his glasses with a grubby handkerchief, doubling as it did for an old paintrag. A black and white dog with one eye missing sniffed around his heels. Harry motioned to kick it. Resisting the temptation to sink its teeth into Harry's leg, the animal slunk off to explore the gutter. Harry wondered how long it would take it to find the remains of the dead cat.

Next door to Nasty's, the heavy bass line of a reggae track pounded out. *'A Babylonpolicyafolicy'* chanted a flat and mournful voice. The volume grew alarmingly as Harry approached. Through a haze of ganja smoke that had certain times of day seemed to envelop this particular stretch of the street, an assortment of brightly clothed and dreadlocked children bounced out of the house. The eldest was no more than seven. They formed a circle around Harry.

'Money missa!,' demanded the biggest boy, holding out his hand. They began to pummel Harry's lower body with their fists, chanting in unison. A downstairs window opened and the space was taken up with a rainbow of colour, a mass of braids and locks as a large Jamaican woman appeared.

'A oo dat a knock pon di door, Ras 'im not 'ome,' she bawled, 'im ain't bin 'ere since long-time so.'

'Ras claat 'im never 'ome,' mimicked Harry, missing the rhythm of the patois by a considerable margin.

'Aint no mi fault mon. 'Im not come round no mo' mebbe. You wan' buy ganja mon.'

Harry indicated that he didn't.

'Then goweh now you dam lagga head.'

Harry's reply that he had come to collect the rent was swallowed up along with the reggae rhythms by the agitated roar of powerful motorcycle engines. The 'Desperados' were revving up their machines with some venom outside number 48. They were wearing full 'colours' They seemed to be off out for the day. Harry was cheered a little by this. It would mean he had one less call to make. Each time he had called at number 48, a different and progressively more menacing ruffian had answered the door. Harry could only guess at how many of them lived there but it seemed to be well into double figures and he had to admit he was terrified of each and every one, more so even than he was of Nasty. This was not the basis for a successful landlord-tenant relationship.

Harry glanced at his clipboard. This must have been instinctive for he needed no reminder that he had collected no rent on this particular morning. He turned over a few pages as if playing a game with himself to see who owed the most rent. If so, there was no doubt about the outcome of such a contest, for in the three years he had lived in Slumpton Terrace, Nolan Rocco had paid no rent at all. Nolan Rocco was the bane of his life. If Harry could find a way to get rid of Nolan Rocco he would be able to put up with all of life's other disappointments.

The Tacklers' had a new board nailed to their front window. Already it had been daubed with offensive comments. Roy Tackler had once been a footballer. Scoring four own goals in Slumpton United's 4-3 defeat to Arsenal was the only time however that Roy made the headlines. Without his dubious contribution, Slumpton would have made the semi-finals in the cup for the only time in their 95 year history. What made matters worse for Roy was that the fact that his last two own goals had come in injury time. After 90 minutes his side had miraculously been leading 3-2, when Roy's mistimed overhead kick surprised goalkeeper, Gareth Garry, and went in the top right hand corner of the net. This was reprised two minutes later by his backwards header into the top left hand corner. He was summarily dismissed by his club. After this, Roy gave up football. He tried his hand at a number of occupations, failing, sometimes dramatically to fulfil his potential in each one. He now lived here. Even his long-suffering wife, Deidre had left him, Harry had heard recently.

Harry reminded himself of Slumpton United's brief glory days before the FA had closed the ground. Slumpton United had nearly been promoted to the Third Division. He prided himself that he could still name the entire first team. Slumpton was a place on the map then. There were three cinemas and a gymnasium, where you could learn to box. Slumpton had had a thriving Sunday morning market , one of the most prestigious in the city. The dog track that now was only of interest to those dumping toxic waste had once attracted thousands every Thursday and Saturday night. There was hope on the horizon then for residents of the borough of Slumpton. There were bingo halls - and pubs that still had a licence. And there were several Jewish tailors. Now, what was there? Prostitution, all night blues, boarded-up shops, the longest dole queue in the city. - And the likes of Nolan Rocco. But Nolan Rocco was another story.

A Police siren struck up from across the car park. It was still euphemistically thought of as a car park, although it had fallen into disuse and become a rubbish tip of some renown. Cars no longer parked in Slumpton. Taxis refused to take fares within several blocks, and even Police cars could not be left unattended. Harry had been around long enough to remember the days before the riots when Slumpton was 'up and coming.' It had not always been a no-go area.

Harry sidled down the street, examining the graffiti on the walls of the houses - and blocks of flats, these run by the Slumpton Squatters Estate Agency, Harry's only serious rival in the area. Even graffiti was subject to declining standards, he reflected. What had become of the imaginative daubings of yesterday? - gems like 'IS THAT A LADDER IN YOUR STOCKINGS OR THE STAIRWAY TO HEAVEN' and 'PLAIN CLOTHES DRUG DEALERS ARE WORKING IN THIS AREA'. Now, what graffiti there was was monochrome and unimaginative. It was all 'SHARON SHAGS' and 'FUCK OFF HOME PAKIS' And here was a new one 'HARRY LUKER IS A FUCKING CHILDMOLESTER.' It was all so personal. He reached number 52. Cats had attacked the black bags outside and their rubbish was strewn across the pavement. A rusty bin full of holes and minus lid stood beneath the window, its contents incinerated. Arson was one of the major pursuits now, Harry reflected - that and ram-raiding, except the latter was already in decline since there was nothing much left to ram-raid. Harry looked up. The guttering had detached itself from the upper part of the house and hung groundwards like a drainpipe. The drainpipe had long since gone and there was a slimy green stain all down the wall. There were few unbroken windows. The odd thing was that Tardelli did not seem to mind the squalor. While other tenants would tackle him periodically about repairs, Tardelli never did. He differed from his other tenants in every way. For one thing, insofar as Harry could judge, he was educated. What was it Tardelli had told him he did when he had met him in *The Builders Shovel* public house on the night the O'Niells were arrested? Write film scripts? Tardelli had charm and charisma, rare commodities in these parts. Why then did he choose to live in such a slum? And even sometimes pay rent - after all few others on the street seemed to bother with this nicety.

'Tardelli,' shouted Harry, for the front door such as it was was already open. 'Tardelli,' he shouted again as he peered inside into the gloom. In the hallway stood a huge dresser, which housed a collection of stone jars and old stained glass bottles. On the floor was a tall pile of yellowed newspapers and a couple of open holdalls that appeared to be full of dog-eared paperback books. The walls, where they were visible were painted a dark brown and one or two cheap Indian dhurries hung from them. A sour and musty odour hung on the air. It reminded Harry of his National Service days in Singapore. An inside door opened and the sound of an operatic tenor singing a Puccini aria floated through. Tardelli emerged from the shadows, a tall, lean, almost skeletal figure with dark Indian features and slicked-back hair, which even in the half-light was noticeably greying. His style of dress seemed to belong to a younger man. His blue jeans had reached the peak of their fade and were almost white and he wore a pink T-shirt with the logo 'I HAVE NO IDEA WHAT YOU ARE TALKING ABOUT' emblazoned across the front. A red silk scarf was tied around his waist.

'Harry,' he beamed. 'How nice. Come on in.'

Harry followed Tardelli along the hallway. He was of a broader physique by far than Tardelli. He edged himself carefully past the dresser and a pile of cardboard boxes full of assorted bric a brac. He ducked beneath the painted alligator skin and found himself in a room piled high with sundry lumber. The walls were decorated a la Jackson Pollock, although it could be argued without the artist's flair. A black corduroy blind over the window kept daylight out with a vengeance and the room was lit by oil lamps. A large black paraffin stove heated the room - unsparingly. It probably heated the whole block. Harry's eyes nervously explored their surroundings, as he tried to establish where he was, even who he was and what he had walked into. After all, he and Tardelli had in the past always conducted their business at the front door. The room that they were in was or probably had been the kitchen, but with so much disorder, it was difficult to tell. There were no pointers, like cooker, fridge or food. The room certainly fulfilled no culinary function. With a graceful gesture or at least without the use of his fist, Tardelli led Harry through to another room. This room too was dark but at least the walls had been painted red. On the floor a stone sink was filled with water with guppies swimming in it. The sink itself was painted luminous green. An abnormally large ginger cat was lapping up what appeared to be blood from an intricately sculptured bowl on a marble slab, balanced, precariously on a purple trestle table. Papers were scattered everywhere. A cuckoo clock was stopped at twelve o'clock.

'To what do I owe this pleasure?' Tardelli enquired, picking up a bag of carrots and handing one to Harry.

'You seem to owe me some rent,' said Harry, as he wondered what to do with the carrot.

'It's a carrot. You eat them,' laughed Tardelli, for he could see that Harry had not come across such a vegetable in his travels.

'Yes. A carrot.' agreed Harry finally.

'You seem tense Harry. Loosen up.'

'You don't have to collect rent in the Terrace on a Saturday,' offered Harry by way of explanation.

'And neither do you, Harry. You choose to. If it upsets you, don't do it.'

'That's all very well'

'Look! How do you think I manage to live round here? Do you think I'm completely insensitive to my environment? Do you think I don't notice how bad things are?'

'You seem not to.'

The tenor had given way to a soprano. The music was, Harry noticed, coming from an old radiogram in the corner of the room, underneath a large poster of Ayatollah Khomeini, holding a 50p piece aloft.

'For the gas meter,' explained Tardelli, for he could see that Harry was puzzled. 'I'll tell you my secret, Harry. I fantasise. I put my fantasies into writing you see. I create my own world. This way, dreams can come true. If you could, what would you have happen in your life right now.'

Harry considered the question for a moment. His fingers played almost instinctively with the papers on his clipboard. Taking the piss was one thing. A slum landlord had to be used to people taking the piss. But three years. And after all he, Harry had done for him. Not to mention the business with the O'Niells. If, if only - he would be able to put up with all of life's other disappointments.

'It can happen, Harry. Take my word. But perhaps you may not need to take my word. Now! About the rent. I can let you have some next week when my advance arrives. Is that OK?'

'I suppose it will have to be. It's the nearest I've come to a result today,' Harry whimpered, pathos not absent.

'Don't be so negative, Harry. Loosen up. When you step out of here, you are the master of your own destiny. The author of your own script, Harry. If you believe in, in well in almost anything at all then something will happen........You'll see.'

With an air of despondency and a marked feeling that Tardelli too was taking the piss, Harry negotiated the obstacle course to the door and stepped outside.

A profound feeling of time disorientation hit him in the way it did after a lunchtime session at the *Shovel*. Perhaps Harry felt, more like the time he had been spiked with acid when he had collected rent from the Dohertys on the night Boozy Farrell was arrested. The street seemed to have altered somehow, it seemed less hostile. He thought he could hear birdsong. Surely a songbird could not have found its way to Slumpton. There were no trees. A brass band seemed to be playing, although it was rather a dull tune, with just the two notes.

Slowly as if he was coming to consciousness after a dream, Harry began to notice that a large crowd had gathered a distance down the street. Two police cars and an ambulance were parked. Outside Nolan Rocco's in fact. Harry watched spellbound as a stretcher bearing the body was carried slowly out to the waiting ambulance. It couldn't be ...... could it?

# Isn't It Good, Norwegian Wood

Rubber Soul is my favourite Beatles album. It is the album in which John Lennon raises his game. *In My Life* is surely one of the most perfectly crafted pop songs ever, *Girl* is sublime, and still there is the enigmatic *Norwegian Wood*. Norwegian Wood with its veiled imagery describes a clandestine affair that Lennon is having. Biographer, Philip Norman claims in his Lennon biography that the song's inspiration is in fact, German model, Sonny Drane, Robert Freeman's first wife, who used to say she was from Norway, when she was in fact born in Berlin.

I am looking at the Robert Freeman's famous cover photo for Rubber Soul, one of a collection that line the hallway at Florian and Rhonda's house in Hanover Hill. The photos, taken in late 1965, capture the Fab Fours's weariness as their fame and hectic touring schedules becomes overwhelming.

Florian and Rhonda's house in Wellesley Crescent is the last in a terrace of *First-Rate* Georgian town houses. Hanover Hill's fashionable avenues, lined with London plane trees, give the area an air of elegance, and the Repton-designed park which was originally used as a run for horses, still boasts the trappings of its earlier prestige. Monuments and statues to the great and good populate its freestone crescents and circuses, and blue plaques abound. Desirable, substantial, imposing and stunning are among the adjectives you might find in Hamilton and Prufock's window to describe the properties here, along of course with Grade 2 and Listed.

Florian and Rhonda are old friends from my days at the Royal Academy of Music. Although our fortunes have over the years pulled us in different directions, we have kept in touch. Having finished tuning a vibraphone in the area, I have called round to see them on the off-chance they might be in, and have been let in anonymously by their entryphone.

My partner, Sara is less than enthusiastic about Florian and Rhonda. She feels they are too intellectual. Sara prefers the company of more down to earth couples like her friends, Wendy and Wayne or Amanda and Adam. She likes to have a diary of firm arrangements, such as dinner parties or theatre visits. She does not respond well to many of my impromptu suggestions, so I have adopted the policy of leaving her out of the loop on occasions that I want to do something a little spontaneous.

'Hello!' I call out. 'It's me, Jon.'

There is no reply. I pop my head around a couple of doors. Florian and Rhonda are eclectic in their tastes, mixing styles with what they term, measured abandon. They see themselves as conceptual artists, and in addition to Wellesley Crescent, rent a warehouse in Hartwell, which they use as creative space. They could never be described as predictable. In the first room an Indian sits cross legged quietly playing the sitar. He does not look up. The second houses film sets that might have belonged to Terry Gilliam's Brazil, and the third, Florian's model railway. I make my way up the sweeping staircase to the first floor. A pair of Palladian plinths with busts of classical figures hovers on the landing with an abstract steel and glass installation beside them in belligerent juxtaposition. I knock gently on the heavy oak door to the right which has been left slightly ajar, and walk in.

Taking up most of the first floor, the room is absurdly large, much larger than I remember it. Its high ceiling and elaborate cornices give it the appearance of a hall or a theatre. The room is in semi-darkness It seems I have arrived in the middle of a film. As I become accustomed to the low light, I look around to get my bearings. Sombre paintings, a curious mix of Dalí and De Chirico, are on display, along with Florian and Rhonda's familiar J. B. Joyce clock, reminiscent of the one at the station in Brief Encounter, stopped for eternity at eleven minutes past eleven. They once explained the significance of eleven minutes past eleven, but I cannot recall what this is. I feel self conscious at not being acknowledged.

I take in the assembly of arbitrary faces, all of which I seem to recognise. They are seated in an informal arrangement of chairs and cushions around the room. This curious collection of random representatives from my past is alarming. Some have aged as you would expect over a period of time, but others are, to my consternation, exactly as I remember them years ago. No sign of their having aged. All eyes are focussed on the giant TV and Home Cinema system. No one looks up as, with an air of trepidation, I sit myself down on a Verona armchair just inside the door. Apart from the intermittent echo of the soundtrack of the film, there is a hush which is disturbingly pervasive. The film is in what I take to be Swedish, but has no subtitles. Is it Ingemar Bergman's *Wild Strawberries*? I wonder. I feel a growing dryness in my throat. I have difficulty breathing. My chest tightens. The whole scene is so out of context I think it must be a dream. It isn't a dream. In a dream you can't feel your heartbeat, and mine is pounding like a hammer.

There is an eerie detachment about all of those present, as if each of them is in his or her own private universe, but by accident rather than design happen to occupy the same space here in this room. They sit alone or in pairs, and the body language of each seems to suggest that they have no connection with the any of the others. But then, as I look around again, I conclude there is no connection. This is not a re-union. These people would not know one another. There would have been no reason for their ever coming together. I am the only link. I know or have known each of them as separate individuals in different areas and at different times in my life. Some I have met through jobs I have had, some through recreational pursuits and others through transactions of one kind or another. Furthermore, I can see no-one here that I would choose to meet in the pub for a pint.

The flickering light from the film illuminates the figures and their faces take on a spectral glow. If Florian and Rhonda are aiming at *strange* they have certainly cracked it. A few feet away from me sitting upright in a carver seat is Bob Scouler, the nerdy systems programmer I worked with at *International Adhesives and Sealants* over thirty years ago, a temporary summer job and well before the toxicity of their products caused a major scandal. Bob is wearing the same grey serge suit I remember, along with the familiar tattersall check shirt and lovat and mauve paisley tie. His haircut, the neat central parting and the sides hanging just over the tip of his ears is from the same era, although even then a somewhat dated look. He has not aged a day. He looks as if he has just stepped out of the office. I half expect him to start talking about his Morris Marina (brown with a black vinyl roof). Are those IBM coding sheets that he has on his lap?

Next to him stretched out on a bank of Moroccan floor cushions is Razor, my son Damien's one-time drug dealer. He used to hang about outside the college I recall. Did Damien still owe him money, I wonder, or is it Razor that owes him drugs? Razor does seem to have aged dramatically. In fact were it not been for the scar across his cheek I might not have recognised him. The original scar, a legacy rumour has it of a 'turf war', seems to have been joined by a companion just below the jungle of gold earrings. He must only be in his mid thirties but with the reds, yellows and greens of the tattoos that cover his shaved head now faded, Razor looks distressingly old.

Bob and Razor are polar opposites. The chances of them being part of the same social group in any circumstances are remote. Florian and Rhonda are perhaps conducting an anthropological experiment of some sort. Or could this gathering be an example of their conceptual art.

Over by the bamboo palm there is the bulky frame of Ray (Marshall) Stax, who I briefly shared a converted railway carriage with in the seventies. Marshall became a sound engineer with a number of rock bands that nearly made it. As I played the piano, I came up with the odd melody for one or two of the bands. I was never credited, but the royalties would not have been staggering had I been, even with *Armageddon*. The NME showed an interest in Armageddon's début single *Don't You Fuck My Dog* in 1976 calling it a *punk anthem*. It suffered from a subsequent lack of airplay and Armageddon faded into obscurity when the following month the NME turned their attention to The Sex Pistols as the ambassadors of punk. I think they took my piano part out in the mix anyway. I recall Armageddon disbanded after the singer accidentally shot himself in the groin. Looking at Marshall, he has not changed that much except that the platforms and flares I remember have been replaced by contemporary cool clothes, screaming with designer advertising. The clothes may have been au courant but his features suggest that he is still in his twenties. I might be looking at Marshall Stax circa 1976, or this could conceivably be Marshall Stax's son, although the Sid Vicious haircut clearly belongs to yesteryear. I make gestures in his direction but I am unable to attract his attention.

Seated on a gnarled banquette, which matches her leathery countenance, is Denise Felch, who was my manager at the local newspaper I worked on as music correspondent a few years back. She is dressed in mismatched browns and reds. I don't know if it is her build (Rugby League second row), but whatever she wears, Denise had the ability to make look like a sack. She seems to be the only person in the room who is smoking and you have to say that she smokes with dogged determination. The light from the screen highlights the nicotine stains on all her fingers and even her spectacles have a brownish tint. The ashtray on the telephone table beside her is full. Denise does not look over and for this I am thankful. My severance pay from *The Morning Lark* was not generous and we did not part on good terms.

Why is everyone ignoring me? Haven't I materialised properly? Or am I out of focus maybe, like the Robin Williams character in the Woody Allen movie?

I spot Colin and Malcolm, the landlords of The Duck, a pub by the river Sara and I often visit on a summer evening for a drink or two watching the boats make their way round the gentle meander. Sara and I were invited to their Civil Ceremony but we agreed that it was not the right social mêlée, although as I recall the real reason may have been that the date had clashed with Sara's amateur tennis tournament. And seated on a Marley two seater here in this room now mulling over a Sudoku puzzle book are Eileen and Mark from Sara's tennis club. Sara seems to be spending a lot of time there lately with her tennis coach, Henrik. I wonder if maybe they are having an affair. Eileen and Mark look as if they would be more comfortable at home with their ceramic induction hob and their range of rice cookers. They of course like everyone else in the room do not seem to notice me.

And my God! There is Ravi from Maharajah Wines, the *offie* where I used to buy my cans when I played sessions at Olympic Studios. He was always open at two in the morning when I finished my shift. Ravi used to call me George, after George Harrison I think. I never asked. 'Got some Drum under the counter George if you are wanting it,' he would say. 'Special price for you on Stella.' Was that twenty five years ago? It seems like twenty five minutes ago. Haven't I just put a can of Stella beside me down? I pick it up and shake it. It is empty. I have been in the room now for perhaps twenty five seconds, but time seems to be playing tricks.

I have never entirely come to terms with the passing of time. The general experience of its passage is that at twenty, it could be likened to a pedestrian able to take in the surroundings at leisure, at thirty an accelerating velocipede, at forty a frisky roadster, at fifty a bullet train, and thereafter a supersonic jet. However there are some puzzling things about the moment, any given moment, being there and then gone and irretrievable that doesn't sit well with the perception of it in one's consciousness. Something doesn't quite add up about the way many things that are important at the time fade into the obscure recesses of the unconscious, while other trivial recollections from long ago survive intact and seem like they happened only yesterday highlights time's inconsistency. I have to keep a detailed diary and refer to it constantly to keep track of what I did and when. I use *Te Neues* art diaries. But even with this record, all that I am doing was measuring change. I read recently that scientists no longer see time as linear, the bad news for us being that they believe our brains are programmed through a process of indoctrination to think of time as linear. We remember things happening in the past, things are moving around in the present, we can plan to do things in the future and we have an agreed upon measurement of time - so the mind gives the illusion of time and continuum. All there is, however, is now and things happening now and moving around. It could be that time is a loop or even infinite, or both. I have been known to espouse, usually after a glass of wine or two, that all time probably exists simultaneously.

I take the soft melting watches in Salvador Dalí's painting *The Persistence of Memory* which I notice is a design for one of the floor cushions in the room, to be a reference to temporal anomaly. Clocks seem to be measuring something but no one knows what. It's not like length. You can point to an object with a real physical reality and say that's one unit in length'. But time is abstract. Cool cushion though! And also in what must be a surrealist set of cushions is Rene Magritte's *Time Transfigured*, (the one with the steam locomotive emerging from the fireplace). *Ongoing Time Stabbed by a Dagger* is the literal translation for the title of the painting, I recall. The distortion of time is clearly a recurrent theme in this outrageous display. I am almost sure the cushion design that Damien's old Geography teacher at St Judes, Miss Jackson is sitting on is Man Ray's *Seven Decades of Man*. And the set is completed by Otto Rapp's *Consumption of Time*. Definitely not a casual buy from Ikea.

Is that Halo, my old jin shin jytsu therapist sipping the green coloured drink? I only went to see her twice – too much mumbo jumbo, but recall a cornucopia of vibrant Berber jewellery from those meetings. I smile at her, and she hesitantly she smiles back, leaving perhaps an opening for conversation, which neither of us take. Again it comes to mind that I seem to know all the people here, but they are, like Halo, bit players in my life. No-one out of this mismatched melée has been a close acquaintance or played a significant role. Any rationality in their being here eludes me. And if for whatever peculiar reason they are Florian and Rhonda's guests, where for Heaven's sake are the hosts?

It takes me a little while to work out the the figure in the blue and white striped blazer and straw hat sitting on a settee in front of an old vellum map of Scandinavia is Chick Strangler. I am more accustomed to seeing him in Lycra. We used to go cycling together on Sunday mornings a few years ago when it became apparent that both of us needed to shed a few pounds. I myself resisted the lure of Lycra for these outings, favouring a warm and comfortable tracksuit. Chick has left the bike in the garage once or twice over the past five years by the look of his girth. Chick and his wife Cheryl lived next door to Sara and me in Dankworth Drive. Red bricked semis on a suburban estate, near the golf course. Last I heard the Stranglers had moved to Florida. A long way to come to watch a Swedish film - which I now notice is displaying its subtitles – in French.

My French is a little rusty but Isak, the old man in the film recalling his life seems to be saying something along the lines of 'I don't know how it happened, but the day's reality flowed into dreamlike images.' I don't even know if it was a dream, (rêve is dream isn't it?) or memories which arose with the force of real events. And then something about playing the piano.'

There are too many big words but I recognise odd phrases, something about a strangely transformed house and a girl in a yellow cotton dress picking wild strawberries. I try to follow for a little while. The old man has found a portal into the past it seems and is trying to talk to Sara, the girl he loved who married his brother, Sigfrid.

The crisp black and white images flash over the faces in the room.

I become aware of Russ Harmer and Dolly Dagger. Have they just arrived or have they up till now been hidden from sight? Russ Harmer was the neighbourhood bully when I was growing up. For years he menaced and beat up anyone who did not suck up to him, until one day he ran into Borstal boy, Tank Sherman. Whether Russ became less odious after the fierce hammering he had taken is difficult to say, but it had knocked his facial features into a shape that remained easily recognisable today. I cannot connect him with Dolly Dagger in any way but here they are together. I shared a house in Dark Street with Dolly Dagger, along with a forever changing roundabout of short term tenants in the months of my post-student malaise. Dolly Dagger was in those days working as an escort and even then it seemed hell bent on a descent into drugs, one which fortunately I did not succumb to. We are not talking a little Blow or even an occasional toot of Charlie here, although that's how it started. We are talking *freebasing* and *needles and pinza*. Despite the decline, Dolly has one of those faces that somehow still retains the carelessness of youth, fine Oriental features you could never forget. She has aged, certainly, but at least she is still alive.

It is a monumental shock to see Bernie Foden who used to service my Sierra. I have palpitations as my heart goes into overdrive. Bernie died ten years ago of throat cancer. I went to his funeral. I close my eyes and open them again. He is still there. This is not a faint apparition, this is a living, breathing, three dimensional human form.

'Bernie!' I venture. He does not reply.

The rupture of logic here in this sinister theatre is stifling. My nerves are in tatters. What on earth is happening here? Am I having a nervous breakdown?

Just when I think the disturbing soiree can get no more bizarre, the actor Dirk Bogarde, who I have never met, drifts in dressed immaculately in a dark three piece suit, Borsalino hat and thin woolen tie. He looks as he did in his matinee idol days. Didn't Dirk die recently too? If so, no one seems to have told him. He breezes over to me and holds out his manicured hand. We shake hands and he congratulates me on something that in the confusion goes over my head. He then switches his interest to the film and sits down next to Razor. Neither acknowledges the other.

This is all too kooky. I decide I have to pull out to go and look for Florian and Rhonda. They will hopefully be able to shed some light on what this surreal circus is all about.

Set over several floors with unexpected half landings and mezzanines and many other changes to what would have been the original design of the house, their home is a bit of a maze. Florian and Rhonda bought the house as a *project* at the beginning of the property boom in the early eighties and have bit by bit converted it. Not in a conventional way by any means. I feel an eerie chill and pull my jacket around me as I explore the photographic darkroom and the embalming suite on the other side of the hallway. Finding no-one there I start to make my way upstairs.

It is by now getting dark and I cannot find a light switch. In fact mounted flush on the wall where you might expect to find a switch is a full 88 key piano keyboard. Do I have to play a note or select a chord to turn on the light, I wonder. I experiment with a few chords, C major and C Minor, D major and D minor then all the other majors and minors. No lights come on. I play Wagner's famous 'Tristan Chord'. 'Disorientating and daring', they called it at the time. It isn't the one though. Still, no lights. Perhaps I need to play a tune. I play the opening bars of What' I'd Say and Imagine. The intro to Bohemian Rhapsody. All a bit too obvious maybe. I try the opening from Blue Rondo à La Turk and one of Satie's Gymnopédies or is it a Gnossienne? I notice that a shaft of light is now guiding me to a room on one of the upper floors.

As I reach the top of the stairs, Anna appears from the room carrying a Rococo style floral tray. She offers me a bagel. Her greeting is one of expectation rather than surprise. Mine is one of surprise. Astonishment!

'Would you like it with cream cheese?' she asks. An amatory smile flashes mischievously.

Anna looks exactly as I remember her five years ago; we had a clandestine liaison when she was married to Bob. Anna has not changed a bit. She is tanned and her hair is cut in the same way in a longish bob cut and even has the same russet red colour. Flame red I think it was called. She has full lips, and eyes that are so dramatically large, volatile, and seductive, so strikingly set, that I wonder if they are real. Her Louis Vuitton skirt hugs her hips tightly and her breasts seem to be powering their way out of the low cut top she is wearing.

Sensing my embarrassment at our meeting she says. 'I don't have the patience for foreign films either.'

We make small talk for a while about the freak thunderstorms we have been having lately and the tabloid sub-editors' strike. I do not want to advertise the full scale of my bewilderment at the series of events unfolding. Here is a beautiful woman I haven't seen for years and I do not want to burden her with my insecurities. Sometimes there can be more than one explanation to a situation.

'What about you?' I ask. 'What are you doing here?'

'I *live* here,' she smiles. 'I rent rooms off your friends Florian and Rhonda. Would you like me to show you?'

She leads me off to her pied a terre. It is brightly coloured and furnished with pine furniture in the Scandinavian style. I sit on a rug. She opens a bottle of red wine to go with the bagels and cream cheese. She slips her skirt off slowly to the sound of a sultry tenor saxophone. Anna has one of those hi fi set-ups you can hear in every room. Stan Getz was always our favourite. The wispy mellow tone of Serenade in Blue is followed by Secret Love,But Beautiful, and Lover Man

When Anna and I return downstairs a little later, the film has finished. The guests all seem to have left and Florian and Rhonda are clearing away.

I ask about the guests.

'Just some people from the film club,' says Rhonda. 'We are looking at the Bergman classic to explore the concept of 'the unreliable narrator.'

'I didn't think you two were there,' I say. 'I could not see you.'

'There were only six of us this week,' said Florian. 'Bit disappointing really.'

I begin counting. 'What about Marshall and Razor, Chick, Denise Felch, Bob Scouler, Colin and Malcolm, Dolly Dagger, Russ, and Ravi. Bernie, Halo, Miss Jackson, Eileen and Mark from the tennis club. And Dirk Bogarde.'

'What?' say Florian. 'Who?'

'They were all here watching the film,' I protest.

'No, there was just myself and Rhonda, Elliot and Rachel, and the Melton Constables,' insists Florian. 'Six of us.'

'Either way, doesn't that prove the point?' says Rhonda. 'At some stage in a story the reader will realise that the narrator's interpretation of the events cannot be fully trusted and will begin to form their own opinions about the events and motivations within the story. After all a story is only a story. It's fiction.'

'What about the unreliable reader?' says Anna.

'The reader isn't the one sending you on a wild goose chase or masking an affair,' says Florian.

'Isn't everyone an unreliable reader though,' says Anna. 'After all everyone brings their own experience into the reading. What if this story is just about Jon coming to see me for a clandestine affair that he is trying to hide from Sara. And none of the rest of the story happens - and you all don't exist.'

'Anyone like a drink?' asks Rhonda.

Anna says that she works in the morning and starts to laugh.

I find the bathroom and light up one that I made earlier. 'Isn't it good, Norwegian Wood.'

Anyhow, I do not think I shall tell Sara.

# North South, East and West

Sometimes, just for a moment, everything seems in place. For this brief spell of time, a supernatural force seems to be at work. There is equilibrium in the universe. It might be referred to by some as an epiphany, an insight through the divine. Here at the top of the mountain, Gregory North finds such a moment. Gregory's mountain may be metaphorical, as might the moment, but briefly space and time conspire to offer him that sentient feeling of arrival. He is where he wants to be. It cannot last. Destiny cannot allow contentment. All actions are bound to burst the bubble.

So, how does Gregory find himself at the summit of the metaphorical mountain? What is his story? Gregory is born into a modest but steady background in a small town in the south of England. From an early age, he displays an inquisitive nature and a creative spirit. He passes all the right exams with appropriate distinctions and wins a scholarship to a revered English university. His tutor describes him as a genius. He quickly lives up to this weighty kudos. He invents a life-saving product that the world needs. The life-saving product not only makes him at twenty five the youngest person to win the Nobel Prize for Medicine, it makes him a multi-millionaire. Money does not necessarily buy you love or indeed happiness, and fame is notoriously fickle. Nevertheless, Gregory meets a beautiful woman who he feels he can communicate with on a spiritual level. He marries her. Fairytales proliferate. Clichés abound. He has his crock of gold. He remains level headed. There is equilibrium in his universe. The fame of a Nobel scientist is low key. You would not know who Gregory was. His name is never in the papers.

Where there is light there must also be shadow. They are interdependent. Gregory might like to stay exactly where he is but life insists on change. Change is the only certainty. Other forces are at work. It can only be downhill from here. There are different paths down the mountain. The west would be the best but Gregory North could go for the east putting himself in peril. The compass points may be metaphorical. The trouble that lies ahead may not be metaphorical.

Crime can take many forms. The view that crime is the province of those that do not have a large enough stake in the system, or that there is some biological or psychological explanation that accounts for deviant behaviour misrepresent the evidence. Criminals lurk everywhere. There is one not far from you now. There are many in the vicinity of Gregory. He is right in the firing line. They want to plunder his ideas, hack his computer, or forge his documents. They want to steal his money, burgle his house or steal his identity. They want to beat him up, burn his house down or kidnap his wife.

The descent begins. Gregory gets a phonecall. He does not recognise the voice. It has been disguised by software called *geocrasher*. You can download *geocrasher* for free. It makes your voice sound like a robot. The robot voice tells him that they have kidnapped his wife. The caller does not specify what the demands are for her safe return. He says he will call later. He tells Gregory he is not to contact anyone about the call and he should not try to trace it. The whole strategy is calculated to cause maximum uncertainty, something that the kidnappers have been working on. This is not something that should be happening to a Nobel Prize winner who has invented a life-saving product that the world needs.

Gregory's wife is Italian. She is called Allegra, which means happy. She is not happy, as she is locked in a windowless space miles away from home. She is being held captive by two ruthless villains. One of them seems to do all the talking. He barks orders at her. His accent is hard to place but may be eastern European. The consonants seem to crowd the vowels. His Heckler and Koch handgun has the look of one that has been fired. He is covered in tattoos and has a scar running down one side of his face. He is disarmingly tall and has to stoop to get through the door. His drainpipe trousers are tucked into a pair of jackboots, somehow making him look even taller. He does not look like he would blend in easily anywhere. The stocky one wearing the camel coloured overcoat with the fur collar and the large white Stetson does not say anything. He just slaps her now and again to establish his authority. His eyes seem to point in opposite directions. His skin is pale, like an albino. Perhaps, Allegra thinks, he may be wearing a mask. She is not sure which of the pair is the more sinister. She is terrified.

Psychology is an important weapon in the kidnapper's arsenal. Abduction can be viewed as a transaction. The relationship is between captor and prisoner, owner and chattel. The captor holds absolute power. He knew the moment was coming. The captive who had no idea the moment was coming holds no power. To show his cards too soon can take away the obvious advantage in negotiations that the kidnapper has. The mechanics of human nature is something the kidnappers have been working on.

Gregory waits for the follow-up call with the ransom demand, but this does not materialise. He waits by the phone. He checks his emails and his social media. He even checks the newspapers, but the Hollywood celebrity divorce and the resignation of the England football manager over match-fixing allegations have kept everything else of the front pages. But even if it got out, it would not be here, would it? Nobel prize winners are not household names.

The finger through the mail comes as a shock to Gregory. This is not what he expected the next step to be. He thought that there might be a phonecall asking him to meet at a remote location with a case full of unmarked notes, as it is in films. This is much more horrifying. He is violently sick. He cannot help himself. It is Allegra's finger. Whoever has sent it wants him to believe that it is his wife's finger. It is Allegra's finger, isn't it? He cannot be sure. It is the little finger of the left hand. It looks about the right size. There is no message to accompany it, but an hour later the robotic voice comes on the line.

'You've got the message, I believe,' says the menacing voice. 'Stay put. Don't talk to anyone. We will be in touch later.'

Gregory attempts a reply but the call ends. How can things have changed so much in just twenty four hours, he wonders.

Allegra has not told Gregory she is pregnant. She was saving it for the coming weekend when they would be away together. They were going to their favourite hideaway, the one that no one else seemed to have discovered. The fact that Gregory does not know she is expecting makes her situation seem all the more wretched. There are two lives at stake. Jackboots and Overcoat, of course, do not know. It would probably up the ransom demand if they did. Allegra has no idea what their plans are. They have not mentioned the reason for her internment or what any ransom demand might be. She is in a dark room, about ten feet by ten feet. The room has a hollow sound. It could also be below ground level. Although she was blindfolded, she recalls going down some stairs when they arrived. She is no longer blindfolded but she cannot see anything except when her captors visit. She can hear them approaching now. She shivers with fright.

Gregory's phone rings. He picks it up. The scrambled voice issues a demand.

'Twenty four hours is not long to come up with five million,' Gregory protests.

'In used notes,' spits the voice. 'None of your bitcoin or electronic transfer.'

'That will be impossible,' says Gregory.

'Each day you don't deliver you will get another finger through the post.'

Gregory mumbles something. He is not sure what he is saying. He has the idea that he needs to keep the conversation going. To what ends, we can only speculate. No-one is tracing the call. The phone goes dead. Black clouds tower in the morning sky. There are distant rumbles of thunder. The forecast is not good.

Gregory takes his portfolio and every form of identification he can muster to his local bank branch. He has never actually visited the bank before. He knows nothing about banking. He is not optimistic that he will be able to liquidate his investments, but he feels he has to try something. His wife's captors seem to be uncompromising, but at this stage, he does not want to risk going to the police. Mr Knock, the bank manager is unavailable without an appointment and he is told there is a three week waiting list. Mr Hater, the deputy bank manager sits him down and bangs on about money laundering. Every question or request that Gregory makes is greeted with a round the houses *no*. Mr Hater is full of suspicion. He clearly knows that something is amiss, but will not come right out and say so. Gregory gets up to leave. He wonders if Mr Hater will call the police as soon as he has gone. He returns to the *Pay and Display* to find his Lexus has been stolen. The rain is torrential now.

Sergeant East seems more concerned about the theft of the Lexus than about Allegra's kidnapping.

'Which model is that, Mr North?' he says.

Gregory tells him it is the Lexus LS.

'Very nice motor, sir. Would that be the LS460 or the LS 600?'

'The 460, but what about my wife's kidnapping?'

'One thing at a time sir. Is that the long wheelbase model or the sport model?'

'How many Lexus 460s do you see on the road round here? Look! You've got everything you need to know you have the registration and the colour and even the chassis number, now what about my wife?'

Jackboots holds Allegra down. Despite her struggles, he begins to force her rings off over her swollen knuckle.

'We need these, lady' he barks. 'I think they might help with our negotiations.'

It is only when they are being taken away that Allegra realises that rings are more than just tokens of affection. They represent her marriage. Everything that Gregory and she have together. Ties that bind in this way are sacred. She experiences the symbolism of the loathsome act that is taking place. It feels to her like murder. She screams. Jackboots covers her mouth with his hand. Her instinct tells her she should bite it. Quick as a flash, Overcoat pulls out his pistol. It is now pointing at her. She has never been more terrified. A trickle runs down her leg.

Jackboots has the rings in his hand now. He holds the engagement ring up to catch the light that filters through the open door. He forms the impression that it is a valuable one. Allegra knows it is a valuable one. It is a single stone Cartier diamond.

'You'll get your money,' stammers Allegra. 'My husband will give you the money - for my safe return.'

'You think so,' barks Jackboots. 'You don't know how much we are asking for, lady.' Overcoat stands there, pistol still raised. Unlike the pistol, his eyes still seem to point in both directions.

'I could speak to him if you like and tell him that I am safe.' Allegra bursts into tears once more.

'That will not be necessary, Jackboots says, a smile emerging from the wreckage of his features. 'He will get the message soon enough,'

Using his pistol, Overcoat motions her over to the back of the room. Without further ceremony, they leave. She is thrown into darkness once more. Things, according to historian Thomas Fuller, seem darkest before the dawn. Is he stating the obvious or is this axiom more profound?

The ring finger with Allegra's engagement ring and wedding ring on it arrives by courier, early next morning. It is freeze wrapped in muslin inside a small cardboard package. The courier does not have the sender's address. He seems a bit vague on everything. Gregory suspects he is not a real courier, but before he has chance to quiz him further he has disappeared on his Honda. Gregory does not have a car to pursue him.

Max Tempo of The West Detective Agency is not what Gregory expects a private detective to look like. *The West is the Best* is the agency's slogan, but the diminutive middle-aged figure with the receding hairline, the crumpled blue linen suit and the red and orange striped sunglasses that the agency has sent does not seem to fit with this image at all. As he introduces himself, Gregory who is six foot tall towers over him. Max cannot be more than five foot two.

'Let's get down to business,' says Max, offering Gregory some chewing gum. 'How did you find out about the abduction?'

'I got home and found a crude note in red marker pen, at least I hope it red marker pen blu-tacked to the fridge. It said, 'We've got your wife! Stay put!''

'Any sign of a struggle?' Max asks.

'Now you come to mention it, no,' Gregory says.

'Could mean nothing. Could mean nothing. Does she have a laptop, tablet or anything? Any sign of her phone?'

'I've looked through her phone, but found nothing out of the ordinary, but laptop and tablet both have passwords.'

'You don't know what they are. Am I right?'

Gregory says he does not.

'No worries,' says Max. 'Let's have a look, we'll be on in no time.'

Max is able to get in straight away. '*John the Ripper*,' he says. 'Great little app.'

In no time at all Max has scanned the emails, recent documents and pictures. Nothing remarkable shows up. This is often what he finds in cases like this. The good detective has to come up with more imaginative methods, he says. Meanwhile, he has wired up a device to record the phone.

Time, of course, is of the essence here. Gregory is impressed with the speed that Max works. First impressions can be misleading. He lets

Max know.

'It's not every day I get a Nobel Prize winner as a client,' says Max.

'How do you know that?' asks Gregory.

'I just sensed it,' says Max, cryptically. 'Now tell me about the phonecalls, and while you're at it show me the fingers. We can get to the bottom of this I'm sure.'

Gregory explains the phonecalls and how he is unable to cash in his portfolio.

Max nods, while he examines the two fingers. He draws no conclusions from these. He is more interested in the diamond ring. Why have they sent it back he wonders when it could be worth a hundred thousand in itself.

'It can mean one of two things, he says. Either they are very confident that they will get the money or they are amateurs.'

It would be difficult for the observer to guess the power relations between Jackboots and Overcoat. Although Overcoat does not, perhaps cannot speak, they communicate effectively. They are a good fit as a team. They operate with a strange telepathy. Perhaps Overcoat has peripheral vision and his function in the team is to be watchful. The observer would not be able to pinpoint their country of origin. Jackboot's accent might make Romania favourite. His tattoos too are in an Eastern European language. If you are looking for sartorial clues, you wouldn't know where to begin. There is something theatrical, perhaps filmic about their bizarre appearance. In everyday life, they would be as inconspicuous as a pair of tarantulas in a bowl of fresh cream. All in all, they are an enigma. The indications are that, as in many kidnapping cases, the motive is money. It is time for Jackboots to make another phonecall. He once again makes it over *voip* using *geocrasher*.

Allegra wonders how it has come to this. How has she moved from her work with Dior and Dolce Gabbana in the high flying fashion world of Milan, weekends on Lake Garda and skiing in Cortina D'Ampezzo to being held captive in this darkened room, not knowing if she will live or die? It is quite a descent. It all started when she came to London for a fashion shoot. How had she come to meet a Nobel scientist? She didn't have the slightest interest in science. She was into the arts. Gregory might cut a dashing figure but perhaps she should have found someone that looked after her better. Why hadn't he come up with the ransom? It was hours since they had taken the rings as a bargaining tool. Why had she fallen for him? Certainly he had a lot of money, but she was not exactly poor herself. The fashion work brought in a decent income. And she gave all this up. They didn't even socialise that much. He was always working on some paper or had a meeting with the board. If he hadn't been working, these two murderous villains would not have been able to just walk in and bundle her into the van. She thinks she has been here now for nearly two days. She is hungry. She has had nothing but water for the duration. Even if she could find a way to relax, she cannot sleep. The room gives off a continuous hollow sound like amplified tinnitus.

'You will have taken delivery of the ring finger,' says the metallic voice. A green light come on Max's device to show it is recording. 'Quite generous of us to return the valuable rings, do you not think. But, my friend, that is all we will be returning till we have five million.'

Gregory says that he is working on this. Max has advised him to do so. He has said that you should never show defiance in such a situation.

'Good! I'm glad you are beginning to see things our way. I expect your lovely wife will be glad too. I will call at exactly five o'clock and we will arrange a time and place to pick up. You will have the money by then I am sure.'

Gregory says that he will do his best.

'I expect you would also like your nice car back too. When you deliver the money, we will deliver your wife in the boot of your car.'

On that note, the conversation ends. The green light on the device changes back to red.

'That was great,' says Max. 'Watch this!

He presses a couple of keys on his device and plays the recording. It is now a proper sounding human voice. '*ModulatorPlus*. Great little app,' he smiles.

The voice, they both agree does sound Eastern European. Max explains that Eastern European languages have consonant clusters so they tend to shorten the vowels when speaking English. To Gregory, it just sounds Eastern European. Max takes a gigantic pair of Sennheiser headphones from his bag to listen more closely. His bag must be dimensionally transcendental, Gregory thinks. He appears to have a whole workshop in there. Max says he is listening for background noise. He closes his eyes in concentration and begins playing with the frequency sliders on the side of the headphones. Finally, several minutes later, he takes them off.

'I think I've got it,' he says. 'The call was made by a mobile phone redirected from an unlisted landline from a blue Ford transit van near a railway station, but what I'm not getting is which railway station or the registration of the van.'

Gregory wonders how Max can tell that the transit van is blue but he doesn't like to ask.

Iancu Emanuel Constantinescu's career as a lion tamer ended when circuses stopped using wild animals. The Romanian International Circus, which had built its reputation on dangerous stunts, folded. Iancu's appearance, the legacy of years of taming ferocious big cats and a long relationship with Silvia Daciana Vacilescu, the circus's tattoo artist, left him with little prospect of getting a job. In a word, he looked scary. He felt he might as well use his intimidating stature to frighten people. Kidnapping seems to be the obvious place to use his skill set. His friend, Dragomir Stan Antonescu had been a clown with the circus. As he was mute, his chances of getting a job when the circus folded were also slim. Dragomir's lack of speech was however compensated by remarkable eyesight. He had long been collector of handguns and was a crackshot. It seemed natural that he should team up with Iancu.

The only way that you can learn kidnapping is by going ahead and doing it. There are no training manuals or kidnapper's colleges. If you get it right, you can make a good living and you do not need to work long hours. Iancu and Dragomir start small by kidnapping a pub landlord in a popular seaside town and asking for £500. They find that this does not cover their expenses. Their next outing is a football manager of a Championship team, where they manage to get £5000. They brush up their technique by watching a number of kidnapping films. After watching Fargo, it occurs to them that it might be a better idea to abduct a partner rather than the target himself. They get £20,000 this way by kidnapping a minor celebrity's wife. They manage to convince the celebrity to pay up when they send him a lock of her hair. Allegra is only their fourth victim. They are thinking of asking £50,000 when they find out that Gregory is an incredibly rich man. He has reaped the benefits of inventing a life-saving product that the world needs. To up the ante, Iancu feels that they need to employ scarier tactics, so he purchases a preserved hand from Stelian Serafim Albescu, a former reptile trainer with the circus who is now working as a mortuary assistant. With so much inexperience the potential for disaster is immense.

'How do we find the blue van and what do we do if we find it?' Gregory asks.

'We follow it,' says Max. 'What we do when it takes us to Allegra is probably the question you should be asking. But don't worry I'll think of something. That's what you are paying me for. Now come on! Let's get to the station. They might still be there.'

'But, you said you couldn't tell which station.'

'Have you any better ideas? Next, you will be saying what if there are two blue vans. There! I've diverted your phone. Now let's get going.'

Max packs his bag, cracks open a new pack of chewing gum and off they go in Max's grey Yaris.

'Nobody notices you in one of these,' he explains. 'Not even with tinted windows. Inconspicuous but fast.'

Allegra's miscarriage is sudden. Jackboots and Overcoat arrive just after it has happened. She is covered in blood. At first, J and O have no idea what has happened. It slowly dawns on them both. She seems hysterical. They do not know how to handle the tirade of verbal abuse she subjects them to.

'$#@!&*^/## $#@$/^ I Need A Doctor,' she screams at them. '$#@! &*^/## $#@$/^&*(())*/$@#: Scum.'

They sense that pointing guns is not the appropriate response, but are not in a position to offer understanding and tenderness. They back off. They can wait in the van. It is parked just down the road by the railway station. They can go back in a few minutes. Allegra, they reason, will have calmed down by then.

Max and Gregory arrive at the railway station car park just in time to see Jackboots and Overcoat getting into the blue van. There is only one blue transit van. They must be the captors. What an odd looking pair they are though.

'How's that for timing,' says Max.

He parks the Yaris a few bays behind the van, in preparation for it driving off. He can follow at a discreet distance. The van, however, does not move. Although the van is fifty feet away, Max manages to rig up a device up to listen to their conversation.

'A friend of mine borrowed it from the secret government base,' he explains.

Jackboots and Overcoat's conversation comes through loud and clear. Unfortunately, they are not speaking English.

'It will come with a translator in a couple of years,' Max says by way of apology.

Only one voice seems to do the talking. It is the same voice that made the phonecall earlier. The one wearing the overcoat and the Stetson seems to be nodding or using sign language.

Had Max's hypothetical translator been operational the conversation they would hear would go something like this.

'Perhaps we should reduce the demand.'

Silence

'Count our losses.'

Silence

'Down to ten thousand. What do you think?'

Silence.

'We can make a bit more on our next job, maybe.'

Silence.

If Max's hypothetical translator had been operational, the substance of the phonecall that Gregory receives on his mobile would not have been so unexpected. As it is, he feels he has been let off the hook somewhat. He is sure that Mr Hater will let him have ten thousand pounds from his assets. Why, he wonders, have they reduced the sum so drastically. It feels like bargain basement.

'Three hours time, that's five o'clock, Used twenty pound notes' says Jackboots, establishing the upper hand once more. 'At the entrance to the disused airfield. Look out for a blue van. Your car will be close by. You won't be able to see your car from the road. Your wife will be in the boot. No funny business or you know what will happen.'

No-one makes a move. Max wants to stay put so as not to lose sight of the villains. Gregory thinks that he should probably be at the bank, but is dependent on Max for transport, and it seems J and O are in no hurry to move business along.

Max has been in stakeouts before. He understands the terrain. A good deal of patience is necessary. You need a cap to pull down over your forehead. And a pack of cigarettes. Gregory is a stranger to the underworld, university did not prepare him for this. To him, the underworld is something that Orpheus got himself into in Offenbach's operetta. Gregory does not have a cap to pull down over his forehead. And he has never smoked. Jackboots and Overcoat sense that they still have a lot to learn. Things are not going as planned. And now a police car has drawn up a few cars away. How long will it be until they spot the stolen blue van they are in, or for that matter the stolen Lexus 460 about a hundred metres away, and who are those people in the grey Yaris? Are they watching them?

Miscarriages can be psychologically damaging. The attachment to the foetus it is said begins very early into pregnancy. Women are often reported to *lose themselves* after such an event. Given the circumstances of Allegra's loss, this might be the expected consequence, but she finds that there are immediate and more profound results of this cruel termination. Her soul has gone, her spirit has parted company with her physical body and disappeared into the ether. When she screams it is not now her that is screaming, but something that is happening as a result of a bodily impulse. She does not inhabit the scream. It is no longer her scream. It is not her who finds that she can push the door to her prison open, where Jackboots and Overcoat have not secured properly. It is not her who finds herself staggering up an unfamiliar street.

She finds herself in the vicinity of a railway station. Something inside tells her she should recognise it, but she can't connect with this part of her. The link has been severed. There are a lot of people about. She spots a blue van and a police car. The police seem to be asking the people in the van to step out of it.

'My God! There's Allegra,' shouts a shell-shocked Gregory, making a move to jump out of the Yaris.

'Stop! No! Don't,' yells Max, grabbing him by the shoulder to restrain him. 'Kidnappers have guns, remember.'

This is a pivotal moment. It could go any way. It depends how competent the police are. It depends how desperate Jackboots and Overcoat are. It depends on whether Max has anything up his sleeve. Certainly Max is aware that the kidnappers would recognise Gregory, but perhaps he should have let Gregory go and talk to the police. Is it his professional pride that is urging against this?

Max seems to have subdued Gregory for the moment and they duck down out of sight. J and O seem reluctant to get out of the van. Allegra lurches on zombie-like and disappears into a throng of people emerging from the station. Gregory and Max's attention is drawn away by a squeal of tyres and a scattering of police officers. In a daring attempt at escape, the blue van speeds off. With a squeal of tyres to match, the police car gives chase. By the time Gregory and Max focus back on the station, Allegra has disappeared out of sight. There are hundreds of people now, jostling one another for position around the station entrance. Why hasn't Max got an app on one of his devices that can find someone in a crowd?

As he and Max dash here and there searching for Allegra in the bustling station, Gregory wonders how he has been subordinated to such fickle fortune. He had risen to elevated heights with so little effort. He had never known struggle. Doors had opened easily. His discovery of a life of a life saving product that the world needed had felt as if it were just plucked out of the air. Fortune had up till now always favoured him. He had not even had to put effort into his dalliances. Allegra had fallen at his feet. What in the world is happening to deliver such a dramatic turnaround?

The station has a staggering seven platforms, each one swarming with restless passengers. Trains are arriving from everywhere. Trains are leaving to go to all points of the compass. Allegra finds herself on one of the trains. She does not know where she is heading. She may be going east or she may be going west. It does not matter to a person who has no soul. People stare at her. They do not understand what has happened. They make up their own stories from the *true life* magazines in their heads. Everyone keeps their distance. Gregory North continues frantically to search the station but cannot spot her. He will never find her. He has lost her. He will continue his way on a train of his own. It will be heading south.

# 2015 – An Odd Space Essay

I will be 119 next birthday. In my lifetime, I have seen the birth of the motor car, the aeroplane, radio and television, domestic power, antibiotics, the gramophone record and sliced bread. Let us not forget the vacuum cleaner, the ballpoint pen, the electric guitar, the microwave oven and the atomic bomb. I have seen the acceptance of Darwinism, the rise of secularism, the collapse of Empire and the provision of the welfare state. Oil and petrochemicals have become crucial resources to human civilisation and transformed the balance of power the world over. Oil, of course, is running out. The peak of oil discoveries was in 1965, and oil production per year has surpassed oil discoveries every year since 1980. One day soon we are going to have a lot of disappointed people. Should we perhaps feel a little guilt about our perfunctory waste and our accumulation of air miles?

When I was born, Queen Victoria was on the throne, most families did not have a bathroom, there was horse-muck on the streets, and in cities, gas street-lights cut through the ubiquitous smog. In the countryside though you could walk for miles in awe of the bucolic splendour. I have seen the landscape change out of all recognition with the green and pleasant land losing out to electricity pylons, motorways, and suburban sprawl. Communication in all forms has been revolutionised. When I was born we had the penny post and the Daily Mail. Now twenty-four hour television, mobile phones, and wi-fi are all things we take for granted. The population of the UK back then was around 29 million. Today it is 64 million. People are living longer. I feel I am not helping.

In life, things change gradually. Except in the case of monumental events, like an epiphany or a catastrophe, you are not aware of it. The changes are so subtle that you do not notice from moment to moment, day to day. Age creeps up on you with clandestine stealth, as months, years and decades slide inexorably by. You can perhaps only measure change through a succession of befores and afters. Even then, time acts as an unreliable witness, leaving you unsure of precise chronology. But this could be something particular to my circumstances; I have lived rather a long time. I have been married four times, to Ruth, Natalie, Marielle and Sakura. For the record, I have to my knowledge twenty two great-great-grandchildren and twenty eight great-great-great-grandchildren, and, no, I cannot remember all of their names.

Music means literally 'art of the muses'. It goes back a long way. Ancient Greek philosophers understood the healing effects that music has on the body and soul. Rhythm and harmony represent a universal language; rhythm the heartbeat, the voice the song. Music has been my inspiration. Through my vocation as a composer and musical coach of some regard, I have had the great fortune to meet many of the people who saw through some of the historic changes over the last hundred years or so.

Not many people know that David Lloyd George was a keen saxophonist. This does not appear in any of the numerous biographies of this most idiosyncratic of British Prime Ministers. The biographers concentrate disproportionately on his political career, with a nod here and there to his Welshness (English was his second language). Not a mention of his musical interests. It was, in fact, I who taught the Welsh Wizard the saxophone, which was at the time a marginal instrument even in jazz orchestras. Lloyd George possessed a natural ability, and could have easily mastered the clarinet, but with maverick zeal, he was determined that he preferred the saxophone. He saw himself as a trailblazer. He bought one of the first Selmer Modele 22, saxophones to come to the UK, and guested in jazz ensembles which, although there are no records of this, played at dance halls in the Manchester area.

'Why did we have to fight the war?' I asked him one day. I had spent a majority of WW1 in Italy with a military band, fortunately well south of the front.

'I will tell you why,' he said. 'Because Germany expected to find a lamb and found a lion.'

'No question of sitting around the table and discussing things first then?' I asked.

' Diplomats were invented simply to waste time,' was his response.

This did not seem like a Liberal view, but I let it go.

Mohandas (Mahatma) Gandhi never really mastered the blues harmonica, but on a visit to London in 1931, he came to me for some tuition. Musicians at the time had started experimenting with new techniques such as tongue-blocking, hand effects and the most important innovation of all, the second position, or cross-harp.

Mohandas felt the harmonica was an instrument associated with the poor, and being able to play it to the starving masses back home would lend support to his great mission.

'History would turn out for the better if our leaders learned that most disputes can be resolved by a willingness to understand the issues of our opponents and by using diplomacy and compassion,' Mohandas said to me.

'It is a shame that history has the habit of repeating itself,' I said.

Mohandas thought this a negative view to take and was optimistic that a new type of common sense would eventually emerge if you kept plugging away.

'We must become the change we want to see,' he said.

Mahatma's teachings were something that stayed with me through the years of conflict that lay ahead. He was only four foot nine but he was a huge and inspirational man. I can still picture him, sitting in the lotus position, his bony fingers clenching his Hohner, blowing for all he was worth. I would have loved him to have been able to play *Hoochie Coochie Man* properly on the harp, but sadly he had to leave to catch his boat back to India for an important fast.

The 1930s are associated with the Depression, but I look back on the decade as a happy time. I married my first wife, Ruth, and my first two children, Darius and Conchita, were growing up. I enjoyed a modicum of success with my work, completing an octet and a jazz concerto. We moved to Pimlico, which then was up and coming. It was a great shame to see the clouds of war gathering at such a positive time, but politicians the world over are a stubborn breed.

World War 2 may never have happened if Churchill has been better at playing the piano. Although he showed some initial promise when he came to me and I took him through a few easy pieces, some early Mozart sonatas and the like, his interpretations of Chopin, however, were clumsy and heavy handed. Winston had what are sometimes referred to as butcher's fingers, not suited to deliver the delicate passages of the *Preludes* and *Nocturnes*. He seemed also to display a disdain for the instrument in the fortissimo passages. On the occasions, I tried to explain this to him he usually stormed off in a huff. He did not take criticism well. His famous *Hush over Europe* speech in August 1938 came right after I told him that he played Beethoven's

*Diabelli Variations* with all the subtlety of a tank commander. He growled something unintelligible at me, finished his Remy Martin and went straight off to the House of Commons. Had he been able to control these rages, he may have backed off a little on his warmongering. While we may now all be speaking German, Winston may have gracefully embraced retirement with his Steinway and his watercolours.

'How did you come into music?' Orson Welles asked me once when he was driving me home after his zither lesson. 'Do your family have a musical tradition?' The year was 1948. Alfred Hitchcock had put Orson on to me. I had taught Hitchcock to play the theremin. To be honest, Hitchcock did not really want to learn but thought he might be able to use the unusual instrument in one of his films. Orson, on the other hand, became a bit of a virtuoso on the zither. I heard a rumour that it may even have been Orson and not Anton Karas who played the soundtrack music for *The Third Man*, which went on to me one of the most successful films of all time.

I did not often talk about my background. It was not that I was particularly ashamed of my humble beginnings, but somehow I felt it destroyed the mystique. I tried to dodge the question by talking instead about my early musical influences, but Orson had a persuasive way about him.

'Are you going to answer my question, god-dammit,' he said.

'I come from a railway family,' I told him. 'Both my father and my grandfather worked on the railways. I came into music entirely by accident. I started playing when I was three on a penny whistle that was left in a railway carriage. It had probably belonged to a travelling navvy. I'm entirely self-taught.'

I explained that I quickly found out I was able to play any musical instrument I picked up. It was like opening a box of chocolates and finding all soft centres. I had what my music teacher at Frank Portrait Infants' School, Miss Schnabel, called a precocious talent. I learned to read music before I could read my Jolly Animal ABC.

I got to know Orson quite well; in fact it was through Orson that I met my second wife, Natalie. Natalie was a nutritionist and had been treating Orson for his recurring obesity. Orson was a large man in every sense and, I'm sure he wouldn't mind me saying, obsessed with his weight. He had flown Natalie in from America to keep an eye on his constitution while he was looking for some film locations in the UK.

Natalie introduced me to the benefits of wholegrain cereal, bee pollen, goji berries and noni juice, all of which I have retained in my diet ever since, and are among the things to which I can attribute my longevity, along with a positive attitude to life, regular exercise and an active sex life. I subscribed to my friend Pablo Picasso's philosophy that a young partner helped to keep you young. Natalie made me feel like a teenager again. She was nearly thirty years my junior. I was fifty three and she was twenty five. Our extended honeymoon took advantage of the opportunities opening up in air travel and took in all six continents. We were stunned by many unforgettable sights; the multicoloured reefs and cays of The Great Barrier Reef, the decorative gilding and marble sculptures of The Golden Temple of Amritsar, the mysterious city of Machu Picchu in the middle of a mountain rain forest, the boat ride through The Blue Grotto Cave in Capri, the summer sun setting on The Grand Canyon, and the great migration of gazelles and wildebeests sweeping across the Serengeti plain in the early morning, to name but a few. But there were less obvious sights that were equally as pleasing. The colourful paddle steamer chugging down the Orinoco, the silhouette of a camel train crossing the Arabian desert, the reflection of the houseboats on the Dal Lake in Kashmir on a Spring evening. Yes, the air miles were clocking up a little, but young love knew no bounds.

Natalie, although she was always modest about this, was also an accomplished pianist. With a youthful ear, she was an inspiration to my music, helping to take it in new directions. The early to mid-fifties represented a productive period; in fact, possibly I was at my creative peak, as my compositions began to incorporate dissonance and atonality. In a few short years, I wrote a concerto for orchestra using a small orchestra as a solo instrument against a larger orchestra, a quintet (four cellos and a flute), a jazz ballet, and a tone poem based on *The Seventh Seal*. I may not have become a household name, but all of these unusual pieces were well received. Miranda Miercoles, Melody Maker's classical music critic, not one that one associates with praise of any sort, referred to my work at the time as, 'intuitive' and 'groundbreaking'. I framed the clipping.

Natalie persuaded me that we should spend some time in America and, as she was from New York, that we buy somewhere in the city. Money was coming in steadily, and we were able to buy a comfortable apartment in Manhattan, on The Upper East Side, close to Central Park. We were within strolling distance of the museums and galleries that were beginning to prosper and the jazz clubs on 52nd Street. One day, while I was in the apartment tinkling away on the ivories, I had a call from an illustrator for a magazine. He drew whimsical sketches of shoes, he told me. He wanted to learn how to orchestrate and had been given my name, I presume by Orson, as I did not know many people in New York at the time. I explained to my illustrator that orchestration had guidelines, but there weren't any rules as such. You learned orchestration mainly through experience, through spontaneous discoveries, and through the teaching of great composers.

'It's very much a hands-on art,' I said. 'You have to be aware of point and counterpoint and of the families of instruments, timbres of each instrument in the family, and of course, tonality, but beyond that it is up to the individual.'

'Good!' he said. 'That's uh what I wanted to hear. It should be easy then.'

'You mean like major for happy and minor for sad,' I quipped.

'Uh yes,' he said. 'Exactly.' He seemed perfectly serious about this being the case.

'I'm not sure orchestration's something I can teach you,' I said. 'What was it that you had in mind to orchestrate?'

'I have a big plan,' he said. 'They say that time changes things, but you actually have to change them yourself. That's uh, what I'm going to do.'

'Well, we can't do it over the phone, can we?' I said. 'You'd better come on over.'

The figure across the threshold had a ghost-like quality. he seemed to be there and not there at the same time. He wore a white suit and a blue and white hooped Breton sweater. His tortoiseshell dark glasses and platinum blond hair made him look a little effeminate. My first impression, as he limply shook my hand, was that he was incredibly shy, but despite this shyness he had astounding charisma. 'Hi, I'm

Andy,' he said. 'Andy Warhol.'

I invited him in and sat him down.

'I'm going to be famous one day,' he said, deadpan.

'How do you know?' I asked.

'In the future everyone will be famous,' he laughed.

'What? For fifteen minutes?' I joked.

I found that Andy's philosophy interesting and some of the things he said had yet more resonance in retrospect.

We finally moved on to the subject of orchestration. I told him that in terms of musical composition Mozart and Beethoven were probably a good place to start. Mozart for his precision and flow and Beethoven for his bold innovations.

Andy felt it might be better to start with Debussy and Ravel because they were more contemporary and therefore it would not take so long to learn.

'You need to be able to put an idea on one side of Letter paper,' he explained.

I asked if he had met the minimalist composer, John Cage. 4'33 consists of the pianist going to the piano, and not hitting any keys for four minutes and thirty-three seconds,' I told him.

'Cool!' he said.

We spent the next session putting together a bullet point list and the one after that at Boosey and Hawkes music store where Andy bought a selection of instruments. He showed no interest at all in playing them; I think they were peripheral to his mission. What he wanted to orchestrate was an Art Movement.

'What is it that inspires you?' Julie Christie asked me at her balalaika lesson one day. We were in my apartment in Cheyne Walk, overlooking the Thames. She had recently finished filming *Darling* and was reading the script for *Doctor Zhivago*, wondering whether to take the part of Lara that the great David Lean had offered her. She had been round to my apartment every day for a week or so to learn the balalaika to help with the role. Most days it seemed the balalaika I had borrowed from the Russian embassy lay untouched. Julie was sensual and intelligent. She possessed a luminous beauty that the cameras loved. The thing is, she was even more stunning in the flesh. She looked sensational in her skimpy chiffon dress. Despite an age difference of forty years, there was definitely a mutual attraction. I wondered if we were going to have an affair. It had been over with Natalie for a while and I had returned to England leaving her and our son, Melchior, and daughter, Melusine, in New York.

'I hear music in the flow of the river, the rain on the window, the clinking of glasses, the hum of late night traffic.' I said. 'I hear music in everything, in the everyday and that is what sustains me. I have a tune in my head the whole day long.'

'Play me your favourite piece of music,' said Julie.

I had lots of favourite pieces of music. I had always dreaded being asked to go on *Desert Island Discs* as I would be hard pressed to make these kind of decisions. What I wondered could I play for Julie? The great violin concertos of the nineteenth century were out of the question, as clearly they needed an orchestra. I could have picked some Bach or some Mozart, but I thought that Julie was hoping for something more contemporary. Bill Evans *My Foolish Heart* seemed apt. Jazz had been a passion of mine for many tears.

Popular music upped its game in the 1960s, with record producers like Phil Spector, George Martin and Brian Wilson pushing back the boundaries of the art. The Beatles, The Rolling Stones and Bob Dylan among others were spearheading a huge social change through pop music. What had once seemed trite now seemed important and vital. By 1965 through music and fashion, London had established itself as the capital of the cultural world. Pop stars, models and photographers were becoming the new elite. Ray Davies was a friend of Julie's and Julie invited me along to a performance The Kinks were filming at Twickenham Film Studios. It was here that I met Marielle, who would be my partner for the next fifteen years.

Marielle was involved with the music business in an anonymous kind of way, the closest I could come to describing this would be, musical muse. She hung around gatherings of musicians and had a mystical presence. She was a polished player with a rare appreciation of the avant-garde. She was someone you noticed; someone who stood out in a room. She was beautiful; with her deep and lustrous eyes and long dark flowing hair, she looked like a Greek siren, without of course the wings. She was twenty one.

Marielle moved in with me right away. For the next year or two, we played host to the pop world at Cheyne Walk, as young musicians dropped by to learn exotic new instruments. Brian Jones and George Harrison were regular visitors, as were some young lads up from Cambridge who called themselves Pink Floyd. I like to think that in a modest way we changed the direction of rock music. It moved away from the established format of two guitars, bass and drums. I appeared, uncredited, on many of the classic albums from that period including *Aftermath, Piper at the Gates of Dawn* and *Sergeant Pepper*, playing dulcimer, tsabouna, musical saw and serpent. I also composed my Vibraphone Concerto and my famous *Trio for Violin, Saxophone and Strimmer* during this time.

The ten years from around 1967 that Marielle and I spent living on Lanzarote I count among the happiest of my life. Undeveloped at the time and certainly minimalist in its colour palette, Lanzarote offered a perfect spiritual retreat. It was a place that the mind was able to focus. Our traditional whitewashed *casa rural* was in an isolated setting, a few miles from the present day resort of Costa Teguise. The artist and architect, Cesar Manrique, lived nearby and was a frequent visitor. His project was to transform the desert landscape, harmonising his vibrant modern design with the traditional architecture and colours of the island. A huge interest in alternative power was developing in the Canaries and through Manrique's civil engineering team we had both solar panels and a wind turbine to deliver power to our house and the surrounding community. We were pioneers. Why not? Lanzarote is, after all, both windy and sunny. The rest of the world it seems have been slow to follow and is still resisting this somewhat obvious solution to our power needs.

Occasionally our mutual friend, Picasso came over from the mainland to see us. Other than this, Darius and Conchita and their respective families came over a few times (grandchildren growing in number and it seemed quickly growing up), and once or twice Natalie brought our children. Mostly though it was just Marielle and I. It was possible to concentrate on the moment, enjoying each minute of the everyday without rushing towards the next. I gradually found a profound stillness take over my being. I felt young and invigorated. Marielle, as many of you who have seen her work hanging in galleries will understand, during this period became a gifted painter of abstract landscapes. As for me, my music began to develop a profound simplicity.

How many Zen masters does it take to change a lightbulb? The cypress tree in the courtyard.

I have always been a great admirer of the French composer, Erik Satie. He called his Dadaist-inspired explorations *Furniture music*. He saw it as the sort of music that could be played during a dinner to create a background atmosphere, rather than serving as the focus of attention. Satie is the link between these early twentieth century Art movements and the work of Brian Eno. Recognising me as a fellow sonic sculptor, in 1975, Brian sought me out and came over for a protracted stay. Together we composed music that synthesised melody and texture. Although the expression, *ambient music* is often attributed to Brian Eno, I like to think that I coined the phrase. Ambient comes from the Latin verb *ambire*, to surround. Our collaboration produced *sonic landscapes*, *atmospheres* and *treatments*. Film directors came knocking at the door. We had inadvertently created the template for movie soundtracks and background to television drama and documentaries for many years to come. If you watch the BBC you will have heard my music many times without realising it.

I abhorred the right wing politics that began to take over the western world around 1980. The decade could be summed up in one word: greed. Why was everyone so blind to the certainty that uncontrolled consumerism would lead to disaster? What was needed was a new set of guidelines with regard to conglomerates, power generation, air travel, transport, and waste management. And a greater veneration of trees. Marielle and I moved to the New Forest.

The politics of the day were reflected in its music. The decade was a singularly poor one. In the 1980s, popular music reduced itself once more to a succession of bland, artless nursery rhymes. Cheap Yamaha synthesisers and drum machines programmed by greedy, tone-deaf computer programmers produced monotonous, predictable, exhaustible and hackneyed three minute jingles. Flamboyant, androgynous models with streaky makeup and spiked hair pranced around in fancy dress to unrelated storylines in fast-cut short films produced by yuppie film directors. It was a case of nice video, shame about the song. Even established rock acts became mainstream and mediocre issuing insipid power ballads. And jazz began to sound like elevator music. How could you have smooth jazz? Wasn't it a contradiction in terms? To be fair, classical music fared no better during the period. With its fetish for dissonance, it became all but inaccessible.

*Zeitgeist* means the spirit of the times, but can also be related to the concept of collective consciousness, which describes how an entire community comes together to share similar values. Was this the explanation for the decline in musical quality perhaps? Subliminally, people had agreed that music was no longer important. It was better to get rich, and quickly.

Tariq Ali had come round for his violin lesson. I put this idea to him. 'What do you think, Tariq,' I asked.

'In times of peace the arts gravitate towards mediocrity,' he said.

'There was no war in the 60s, but there was lots of great music,' I said.

'No war in the 60s?, he laughed. 'There was the Vietnam War. We may not have been on the front line but as a culture, we were involved. Didn't you go on any demonstrations?'

'I was living in Lanzarote at the time,' I told him. 'But I do remember the Battle of Grosvenor Square. You and Vanessa Redgrave were leading the march weren't you'

'That is correct. And Mick Jagger wrote *Streetfighting Man*. But to get back to my point. Do you not recall the famous line in *The Third Man* about the Swiss?' he said.

'Not word for word,' I said.

'In Switzerland they had brotherly love, they had 500 years of democracy and peace, and what did that produce? The cuckoo clock.'

I conceded Tariq's point.

'Perhaps we will have another war soon,' I said. 'There are some mad people in charge.'

'I don't think it will be a war with The Eastern Bloc,' said Tariq. 'Russia is not a country you can invade and occupy. War is about occupation and colonisation. The next war will be against Islamic states, where they can send in an occupying force. And, of course, there's the oil. Iraq's my guess.'

It seems in retrospect that he was right.

The days get longer and the days get shorter. As you get older the heat of summer makes you uncomfortable, so you look forward to the winter, but you can't cope with the long dark nights and the cold, so you look forward to the spring, and your life passes by, with this contradiction. You are getting older, but you are willing the time to pass. Seasons replace one another in a relentless procession, as the northern hemisphere tilts towards or away from the sun.

The planet Mercury, according to Luigi, my barber in Ringwood at the time, has no tilt my and therefore no seasons. Luigi was one of those people who seemed to know everything. He had been a contender on Mastermind. His specialist subject was *String Theory*.

'No seasons,' I said. 'That's good then, isn't it? Why couldn't we live on Mercury?'

'There is a little problem my friend. It has no atmosphere,' he said.

'Not so good for the old breathing then.'

'And its four hundred degrees during the day and minus two hundred at night.'

'Bit hard to get used to.'

'You'll like this, though,' Luigi said. 'Mercury has a large crater called Beethoven which is the largest in the solar system. They have also named craters after Puccini, Verdi, Vivaldi, Schubert, Sibelius and Wagner. It is riddled with craters. You name me a composer and they have probably named a crater on Mercury after him. I'll find out if they have named one after you, my friend.'

He never did find out. Sadly Luigi died when the steering on his Fiat gave out as he was overtaking an articulated truck near Basingstoke on the M3. He was only sixty two. No age at all.

When you reach your eighties, you understandably find that those around you, those you have known or admired, are dying with increased regularity. When you get a call from a friend you have not heard from in a while, you know it is going to be to inform you that someone you both know has died. The receptionist at the funeral directors gets to recognise your voice, as you order wreathes for lost friends and colleagues with increasing frequency, and you start getting Christmas cards from the undertaker. You find you know all the words to *The Old Rugged Cross* and *Abide With Me*, and your copy of The Times falls open at the obituaries. Death is all around. When you visit the doctors with a routine chest infection, you imagine the grim reaper is sitting next to you.

Through the 1980s following Marielle's death from a rare blood disease, I became acutely aware of my own mortality. It became obvious that one day I would die and although I seemed to be in remarkable health I began to speculate on how I would die and when. None of the ways seemed especially pleasant and most involved a protracted period of pain. Cardiovascular disease was statistically the most likely cause for someone of my age, although hot on its heels were cancer and strokes. Then there were lower respiratory infections, tuberculosis and chronic obstructive pulmonary disease. Nostalgia too I found could fuel later-life depression. Don't look back.

Irving Berlin helped to lift my gloom. Irving was a legend and throughout the twentieth century had had a greater influence upon American music than any other one man. If anyone could deliver a pearl of wisdom, it was Irving. I was fortunate to gain an audience with the great man in a stopover trip to New York to see my grandchildren, as he was by then famously uncooperative. I asked Irving his secret.

'Music is the key,' he said. 'Music had been used in medicine for thousands of years. It enhances memory, helps with concentration, and reasoning skills; even better, it boosts the immune system, lowers blood pressure, relaxes muscle tension, regulates stress hormones, elevates mood, and increases endurance. That's what my doctor tells me. And he's older than I am.'

I knew Irving to be in his late nineties, so that made his doctor very old indeed. 'I'd better start writing some music soon then,' I said.

'Another thing', said Irving. 'I presume you've reached the age that you suffer from earworm.'

'Don't think so,' I said. 'It sounds unpleasant, though.'

'Earworm is where the last tune you heard stays in your head.' Irving explained.

'I definitely get that,' I said.

'The secret is to make the tune in your head a happy one, one with happy words. Positive affirmations and all that.'

'What about the old blue musicians?' I queried. 'They seem to all live to be a ripe old age despite all the 'Woke up this morning and my baby had gone' lyrics.'

'What! you mean lived to be 27, like Robert Johnson and Jimi Hendrix'.

He had a point. I was probably being selective. For every John Lee Hooker or Muddy Walters, there was a Blind Boy Fuller or Freddie King.

'Look at me as a living example of someone who keeps a happy song going round in his head,' said Irving. 'It has worked for me.'

'OK, I will try it.' I said.

'At the same time, don't avoid thoughts of death,' Irving continued. 'Remind yourself your death is guaranteed. Facing death should be something that empowers you and heightens your senses. Feel the inevitability of it. Feel the horror of it. And then open your eyes and realise you are now alive.'

It took a little application, but after a while, I arrived at a view whereby death offered an increased opportunity to see what was important. Music of course was as Irving had suggested, the key; this was the way to make my mark. This realisation provided me with motivation. I kept a happy tune in my head and entered a new creative phase. My *Tenor Saxophone Concerto* was popular, as was my *Sextet for Four Pianos, Oboe and Harp*. But the piece that gained the most recognition was my opera, *Gatto di Schrödinger (Schroedinger's Cat)*, which played at opera houses around the world. Who could forget the rousing fortissimo chorus for one hundred voices, 'Il gatto è tanto vivi e morti.'

Tim Berners-Lee may have been considerably richer had it not been for coming to me for lessons on the cor anglais. Having invented a browser-editor to share and edit information and build a common hypertext, the model for the internet, he was faced with a dilemma. Should he patent the idea, or should he put it in the public domain for the benefit of all? In between run-throughs of Schumann's *Reverie for Cor Anglais and Piano*, we discussed the pros and cons of both viewpoints. It may have been my suggestion that the World Wide Web be royalty-free so that networks could adopt universal standards without having to pay their inventors. Someone, he argued, was going to make millions out of the idea, someone like Bill Gates or Steve Jobs, for instance.

'How would you best like to be remembered,' I asked him. 'As a universally reviled figure or as a benefactor to humankind?'

He must have taken my point. The next day, after we had been over Respighi's *Pini di Roma*, Tim seemed to have changed his position, using some of the very arguments that I had used.

'The World Wide Web must have an open standard,' he said. 'Otherwise, there will be incompatible forms of media, backed by Microsoft and Apple and the like.'

I met Sakura at The Saatchi Gallery in St. John's Wood at an exhibition called *Young British Art*. The show featured work by the little known Damien Hirst, Mark Wallinger and Rachel Whiteread, all of who would go on to win the Turner Prize. I had not wanted to see the exhibition after reading the press write-up about tiger sharks immersed in formaldehyde, but a friend whose view I respected told me I had to go.

'Something important is happening here,' my friend had said. 'Damien Hirst's work is an examination of the fragile boundaries between life and death.'

Sakura caught my look of puzzlement as I took in *The Physical Impossibility of Death in the Mind of Someone Living* (the fourteen foot tiger shark in the tank). What was Art? I wondered. Where were the boundaries? Paul Gauguin had said 'Art is either plagiarism or revolution.' I could accept that Art constantly needed to re-define itself. But in my cynicism, I wondered if was just a question of a dealer or curator saying something was important art, a prominent critic supporting him, and collectors with their mega bucks being persuaded.

'The shark is a metaphor for mortality,' Sakura said.

I found myself no longer looking at the unsettling spectacle in the tank. Sakura was a much more attractive prospect for my gaze. She possessed an exquisite beauty. She had long raven black hair, obsidian eyes and rich nut-brown skin with a flourish of red across her cheekbones. Her body pushed in all the right places against the fabric of the tight floral print dress. I was transfixed. I felt a profound surge of well-being. Another bout of rejuvenation was on the way.

I must have come up with some kind of reply, because the next I recall we were eating dinner at Claridge's and, before I knew it, living together. I wondered later if our meeting had not been set up as a blind date. Sakura wondered the same. She had had a phonecall from the same mutual friend it seemed recommending the exhibition. Sakura worked in television. I did not watch a lot of television, so I was not aware of any of the programmes she had been involved with. In no time at all, she suggested writing my biography.

'Have you never thought of writing one?' she asked.

'I don't think I'm famous enough,' I said. In fact, I had many times thought of writing my autobiography, but I was too lazy to start. The project seemed daunting with so many years to cover.

'Everyone knows who you are,' she said. 'But no one knows very much about you. The world is crying out for some insight into your life.'

Sakura had formidable powers of persuasion. The chapters charting my childhood in Louth in the Lincolnshire Wolds were in the bag in a few days. However after the move to North London, sister Susanna joining the Suffragettes, Walter and I going off to war, and Ruth and I marrying, we reached the point where retrieval of memories was becoming more of a challenge. Looking back was becoming vertiginous. It was a long way down.

'You should have kept a diary,' said Sakura.

'I started to,' I said. ' A long time ago. After the First World War....... I think that they may be up in the attic somewhere in an old leather bag.'

Sakura dug them out, four gnarled Evening Standard Diaries from 1918 to 1921, and eagerly began to devour them.

'What do these xs mean?' she asked.

I told her.

'Three or four times a day...... We only make love two or three times a week.'

'But you aren't as young as you used to be,' I joked. She was 46.

'Why did you stop writing the diary after June 1921?'

It was a fair question. Had I had an unexpected illness? Had I sold my soul to the devil? I couldn't remember.

The biography progressed even more slowly documenting the years after 1921. I had some recollection as to when I had met celebrity figures, and I had dates for some of my recordings, but with regards to my personal life, there were no records. All of my contemporaries were dead, and even my children had difficulty remembering with any precision. Either that or they had not wanted to cooperate. None of them had taken well to Sakura. I was able to tie up the big events like the British Empire Exhibition at Wembley (I had been introduced to one of my early heroes, Sir Edward Elgar) and The General Strike (I was stuck in Dover with Aleister Crowley for twelve days), but the devil, as it were, was in the detail. You wait until you are my age and Alzheimer's starts gently kicking in.

Looking back made me question whether the quality of life had changed for the better over the years. We were now able to travel fast over large distances and get information at the click of a mouse, and every year technological gadgets were becoming, smaller, faster, cheaper, and more convenient, but hadn't we lost our sense of wonder? We seem to have sacrificed a fundamental simplicity. The time and effort spent learning how to use our time and effort saving technology raised the question, at what point would the cost-benefit ratio no longer be in support of our technology? When I was a child, listening to someone reading the story of Alice in Wonderland aloud, without the benefit of even pictures to look at, would have filled me with awe. Nowadays, if a six-dimensional, four headed kraken suddenly materialised in a ring of fire in the room in front of a young child, it would engender no surprise, they would probably just see it as a continuation of Doctor Who or Star Trek.

Sakura and I had gone for a walk in the Wolds around this time from Claxby to Wolds Top. It was a clear day and you could see for miles. We had panoramic views of Lincoln Cathedral, the Humber Bridge and the River Trent. We came across a family having a picnic. While they ate their Subway baguettes, the two youngsters played games on hand-held Nintendos, while the parents looked at domestic appliances in an Argos catalogue. I gathered from their conversation, that they were planning on stopping off at the Lincoln branch on their way home. Nowadays they wouldn't even need to do this. They could buy the Dyson online from their smartphone or tablet.

'Do you ever regret parts of your life?' Sakura asked. She was still working on the biography.

'Of course!' I said, not going down the Edith Piaf or Frank Sinatra routes. 'Many things.'

'If you could live your life over again, what would you change?' she asked. Sakura was not by nature a jealous woman, but I think she may have wanted me to say that my marriages to Ruth, Natalie and Marielle had been a mistake. I didn't take the bait. If there was one thing I had learned about women, it was that each wanted to be the only one you had ever thought of. Apart from which, Ruth and Marielle were both dead, and Natalie, who I hadn't seen for thirty years, would be in her seventies.

'I would get up earlier and I would take more time to smell the roses,' I told her enigmatically. The biography stalled a little.

One morning I pulled back the curtains and saw a ball of bright light blazing brilliantly in the Southern sky. I was mesmerised. I began to understand how the expression, 'bright as the morning star' came about. The man in Jessops told me that what I was seeing was Jupiter and, what I needed was a *Celestron 8 inch Schmidt-Cassegrain* computer controlled telescope. He just happened to have one in stock. It was simple to operate, he said. I would be able to use it right away to discover the delights of star-watching. Once I got it home, I did not find it at all easy, and it sat in the conservatory unused for several months. I had an arts background. I had never learned even the basics about the universe. Finally, with the help of *The Beginners' Guide to the Cosmos,* I began very slowly to pick things up.

Each of the billions of stars that I now had access to through the telescope was another sun. The problem was that there were so many of them and I had no idea where to look. After a crash course in constellation spotting on the Internet and the acquisition of a circular star chart called a planisphere, I was able to identify the ever present Plough and use this as a reference point. I was able to distinguish an endless array of spectacular celestial sights. I could now see Jupiter up close, with its four largest moons, Io, Europa, Ganymede and Callisto, strung out alongside it, Saturn and its unmistakable rings, the forever changing crescent of Venus and the fiery red of Mars. I was also able to see distant nebulae, star clusters and the Great Andromeda galaxy that lies about two million light years beyond our own galaxy, The Milky Way.

For my hundredth birthday, I hired the planetarium. Astronomers like Patrick Moore and George Smoot might not be everyone's ideal party guests, but the after dinner conversation is not dull. I learned that our sun is four million times as big as Earth and produces so much energy, that every second the core releases the equivalent of one hundred billion nuclear bombs. Also that a supernova is a luminous stellar explosion that occurs when a massive star dies, releasing a huge amount of gamma rays, which can outshine an entire galaxy. After the supernova, the once massive star becomes a neutron star, white dwarf, or if it is large enough, a black hole. Black holes are so dense and produce such intense gravity that even light cannot escape. The *Universe* I was told is at least 150 billion light-years in diameter. We are talking really big numbers when it comes to space. The scale of it forced me to reconsider my definitions for large; the word that came to mind was *astronomical*. There were other fascinating disclosures. A bright star which appeared over Bethlehem two thousand years ago suggested the date of Jesus's birth as June 17$^{th}$, not December 25th. The *star* was a magnificent conjunction of the planets Venus and Jupiter, which were so close together they would have shone unusually brightly as a single sudden beacon of light.

The relationship between music and the cosmos probably began with Holst's *The Planets*. The work was composed around 1914, just ten years after The Wright Brothers' first powered flight, and Holst had no idea what was going on out there in space. Little more than fifty years later, we had landed a spacecraft on the moon. The piece of music always associated with this momentous event is Richard Strauss's *Also Sprach Zarathustra*, which was also used in Stanley Kubrick's equally important film, *2001: A Space Odyssey*. The Voyager spacecrafts launched in 1977 contained sounds and images selected to portray the diversity of life and culture on Earth, intended for any intelligent extraterrestrial life form finding them. The music included Bach, Mozart, Beethoven, Stravinsky and Chuck Berry. These have left the Solar System and are now in empty space. In around 40,000 years if things go to plan some unsuspecting alien will be playing air guitar to *Johnny B. Goode* or singing along to the chorus of *My Ding a Ling*. More recently, in 2008, NASA beamed The Beatles, *Across the Universe* at the speed of 186,000 miles per second towards The North Star, just 431 light years away. Time is not on my side, so I am going to have my entire back catalogue beamed to Enceladus, a moon of Saturn, which Stephen Hawking (who incidentally was hopeless on the accordion) informs me, is the most likely place we might find life in the Solar system. This I am told will take a mere 76 minutes.

It is often said you can tell you are getting old when policemen start to look younger. To me, even Chief Superintendents have had the appearance of callow youths since around the time of the Notting Hill riots. I have now had eighteen telegrams from the Queen, and still I can't help but think of her as the little girl stroking the corgi dog on the Newsreels that accompanied the double features in the 1930s. Saga Holiday adverts seem to me like they are advertising 18 to 30 romps. But there are benefits to being old. As Mark Twain said, 'Age is an issue of mind over matter. If you don't mind, it doesn't matter.' It is best perhaps to think of youth as a malady from which we all recover. Old age isn't so bad when you consider the alternative.

Lately, there are signs that our 400,000 year tenure of Planet Earth could be coming to an end. Earth may not be able to support the prodigal violations of our stewardship. The forest fires that raged for months in Australia this year were the worst in history, finally doused by storms of biblical proportions, bringing in turn the worst floods in history. The oil well fires that burned in the Middle Eastern conflict clouded the sky for months so that no crops would grow in seven countries in the area. Bangla Desh was reclaimed by the ocean, after all the rivers that drained the Himalayas cascaded into one. Fourteen million people died in the famine in the African country no one knew was there. I see on the news this morning that an iceberg the size of France has just detached itself from Antarctica. It's all happening. As the writer Kurt Vonnegut said, 'Dear future generations: Please accept our apologies. We were rolling drunk on petroleum.'

What will tomorrow bring? The answer is up to you. It doesn't matter much to me. I will be 119 next birthday.

# STRINGS

The goat is not supposed to be in the house. My daughter Jessica has let it in with the cats. Properly speaking, we only have one cat, a ginger tom called Thomas, but Jessica is of an age that she likes animals, her enthusiasm fuelled by a plethora of Animal Hospital programmes on TV. There are a lot of cats in the neighbourhood and one by one she has taken to adopting them. In retrospect, I shouldn't have read her 'Six Dinner Sid' so often when she was little. She entices the cats in with pouches of gourmet cat food that she puts in the basket when we do our shopping. The goat I think has been attracted by the neighbours' overgrown vegetable garden.

There are not supposed to be any animals in the house according to the tenancy agreement, which for the most part is a standard short let tenancy agreement; I am not permitted to sub-let, smoke, decorate, hold parties, use the property as a business address, etc. Additional clauses stipulate that I am required to raise the Union Jack on a flagpole on patriotic saints days, VE Day and the Queen's birthday, and sound the air raid siren at midday every Saturday. My landlord is called Raif by the way and he likes to dress as a Naval Lieutenant.

I am putting the goat out into the back yard when I first notice something odd. I am putting the goat out - and it seems driving to work in the city, simultaneously. 'I expect I will wake up in a minute,' I think..... I don't. I am already awake – and so it seems is 'the other.'

'What in the blue hell is going on?' I wonder. 'There are two of me.' It feels as if I have split, or multiplied. I am in two places at the same time. My attention moves from goat to car and car to goat. I can see from the outset that this is going to present a colossal challenge to my multitasking abilities. And shatter my reliance on logic and reason. Given that I have not taken any hallucinogenic drugs since my youth, and do not have a history of psychosis, this is a troubling insight.

My car is painted lilac. I can't decide whether it is comforting or unsettling that all the other cars on the streets are painted lilac too. This distraction causes me to drive through a couple of red lights on my way to work in the city. I, that is the second I, the one that is not putting out the goat, do not seem to have got to grips with the complexities of chromatics yet. To add to my state of confusion, the radio is locked into a Russian radio station and the hazard lights will not turn off. And there is a large red spider on my shoulder. With a careful swipe, I get rid of it with a copy of 'Mojo' that I find lying on the floor.

Despite my being acutely disorientated, the car seems to know where I am heading. The route I am taking is instinctive. I am not making navigational decisions. I pass familiar landmarks: the Liebeskind Tower, the Lennon Monument, the billboard advertising John Cage's '4 Minutes 33 Seconds scored for Full Orchestra' at the Orange Theatre, the tattooed bridge, the sculpture of the bungee jumper, the SKB (Smith Kline Beacham) Superstore..... I come this way daily. I work for a company called Alpha Pigeon and we publish computer manuals and telephone directories. Taking the sharp left into Coppola Avenue, I lose the police car that has been on my tail since Bunuel Square. I can hear the siren fading as having missed the turn it carries on along Besson Street. Burl Finch, a town planner a few years ago was a bit of a film buff, in case you are wondering.

The telephone rings. It takes me a little time to find it as it is buried among a pile of sweaters that some of the cats are lying on. I have reset the ringtone to a new tune, and I am trying to recollect whether it is Delibes or Cantaloube. I have a large collection of classical music, so I feel I ought to know. ..... or Puccini.... I am still speculating as I pick the phone up.

'Hello,' I say.

'Hello,' says a woman's voice in an accent I can't quite place. There is an echo on the line as if the call might be coming from far away. 'Is that Mr Stewart?'

I say that it is.

'You are being prosecuted for crossing a fence.'

What on earth is she talking about? She does not elaborate. She just says that her name is Chandra and I will be getting a summons in due course.

I arrive at Alpha Pigeon striking a stocky blue badger as I drive through the avenue of yuccas into the car park, the beast evidently camouflaged by the blue and white chessboard pattern of the tarmac. I cannot remember badgers in the car park being usual at AP, blue badgers perhaps even more surprising. But then I am in a state of shock and disbelief about everything. I move the badger's body onto a pile of telephone directories that we threw out last week (printed with duplicate sections under the letter C) while I go to find a black bag to put the badger's body in. When I return the body has disappeared. It has started to drizzle and the car park is now a mottled violet.

I find the local directory and look for the number of Citizen's Advice. There is no number, in fact, no listings at all under the letter C, so I look up the number for Stipe and Juttner, Solicitors instead. I am not sure how to approach the enquiry, as Chandra did not mention on whose behalf she was calling. I just feel it would be helpful to talk to someone about the summons.

A woman answers the phone at Stipe and Juttner introducing herself as Coral. She asks how she can help.

'I wonder if you could tell me, what does crossing a fence mean? Is it some kind legal vernacular?' I ask her.

Coral has not heard of 'crossing a fence.' Do I perhaps mean a crossing offence? A crossing offence might relate to a traffic violation. She adds that she has a legal database on her computer and she can do a search.

The search draws a blank.

At lunchtime, I leave the office and take a walk up Zimmerman Hill to clear my thoughts. I have felt oddly vacant all morning as if I were in the process of being disassembled. I have felt as if I was somewhere else, or even someone else. Several times in the middle of phonecalls, I forgot who it was I was talking to and had to ask. In fact, at times I was not sure who it was that was talking to me. I found my voice coming out with words and expressions I never used. Something very strange was happening to me. I remember that a little while back my neighbour Mystic Mike said to me, 'whatever it is you're seeking won't come in the form you're expecting.' This had seemed very cryptic, but Mike often spoke in riddles. Without being specific, I was looking for my life to change. I hoped this change would come in a more conservative form, a gentle progress from where I was to where I would be. Something that was more planned, where cause and effect were at the same party. Something that I had some influence over like changing jobs or moving house. What I am now experiencing seemed more like schizophrenia.

At the top of Zimmerman Hill, you look down on several red-bricked blocks of modern apartments at a lower level. These have decorative cream bricks cut in to great dramatic effect. The blocks are staggered in their elevation, and across their flat roofs, you get a spectacular framed view of the city. One of the lower roofs has a garden with a variety of tall ornamental grasses, which make stunning patterns against the sky. I take the spectacle in, breathing deeply to calm myself. Fluffy white clouds drift across the sky like childhood memories. It is quiet, with just a faint hum of distant traffic. A man in a dark suit and a black trilby with a yellow band comes into view. As he passes me he politely takes off his hat by way of acknowledgement. I feel a strong sense of déjà vu. Although this is an unusual colour for a hatband, I myself wore such a hat many years ago. I can remember wearing it on the occasion that Juanita introduced me to her eccentric family in a tumbledown old house with no furniture. A couple of de Chirico prints hung on dusty magnolia walls, These were the only decoration. It was an embarrassing occasion. The family were huddled around a television watching an old episode of 'The Prisoner.' I cannot recall having worn the hat since then. I think I may have left it there.

I walk slowly back down the hill and back to the office via Painter's Lake. In the past few weeks, this has been transformed from classic 'Capability Brown' into a sharp angled post-modern creation. Building work is going on in earnest on the far side, the sound of this muted by the large sheer waterfall that has been constructed. A barn owl sits motionless in a tree. Barn owls are only seen at night, and this is the middle of the day. I have the strange sensation that I am being watched, but I also feel at the same time that I am the one doing the watching. It is a very disconcerting feeling.

Although Raif bangs on constantly about the importance of testing the air raid siren, he does not bother much with health and safety in the house. The gas equipment for instance would horrify an inspector. Sometimes the pressure is up and you nearly burn your arm lighting a ring and other days the pressure is down and it takes nearly an hour for the kettle to boil. On this particular morning, it is up. I nearly burn my arm. After I have adjusted the pressure on the gas supply to a level that I feel will be safe to use, cleaned up the yard, and tethered up the goat, I make myself a couple of slices of toast and a cup of honeybush tea, and put my feet up to catch up with the news on TV. In the aftermath of the assassination of the England football manager, it seems a slow news day, so I flick through the channels. I settle down to watch a programme on 'Waterfalls' on Discovery 3. I have recently had the full cable package installed largely through the persistence of the DigTel representative who insisted that I would save large sums on my bills. He did show me the figures, three or four times as I recall. On DigTel rep's fourth or fifth visit I relented. I now have 200 channels to choose from – and can get 20 megabyte broadband on the laptop and make unlimited calls on the phone. The programme on 'Waterfalls' appears to have traced the history of their construction in parks and gardens in the UK and in summing up is now showing recent examples. One of these is in Painter's Park, not far from where I live. Only recently I took the dog for a walk around there (I forgot to mention the dog earlier in the pets inventory. He is a teacup schnauzer and he is called Albert). Seeing Painter's Park on the television brings about a second wave of detachment, the same feeling I had that morning when I felt I had split, or multiplied.

To add to my bewilderment on Discovery 3 a programme on 'Synchronicity,' is just starting. Synchronicity is used to describe an apparently meaningful coincidence in time of two or more similar or identical events that are causally unrelated. The presenter gives an example, which I feel seems a little weak, if not downright pretentious. He was riding in a crowded car with friends one evening, debating about whether or not to speak on the topic of Infinity for a group the following day. As they got out of the car, he stepped on a string that was in the shape of a figure 8, the infinity sign in mathematics. They all stopped and stared in amazement. He gave the talk, and it was well received.

Outside Alpha Pigeon, on the pavement, four men dressed in ecclesiastical robes stand facing one another in the form of a cross. They have ceremonial staffs and seem to be performing some kind of a ritual, chanting something unintelligible in low voices. One of them is swinging an ornate thurible and a powerful smell of incense hangs on the air. I think; surely this sort of behaviour should be confined to within a church. I pull my collar up and pass them quickly without turning my head to look round.

Back in the office, I feel disorientated. Someone else's consciousness seems to be cutting in like a crossed line on a telephone. I find myself thinking about going to do some work on my allotment, walking the dog, picking my daughter up from school, things that have no place in my life. I do not have an allotment, or a dog, or a daughter at school. Concentration on work is impossible.

'Are you all right, Mr Stewart,' says Candice bending over my desk. 'We've been a little worried about you.'

There is a knock at the door. For some unaccountable reason, I think it might be four men dressed in ecclesiastical robes. But it is my friend, Jack. Jack tells me that he is having trouble with the Internet. He logs on, type in an address, let us say 'ebay,' and this opens up dozens of windows and each time he closes one down it generates another two.

'I have the same problem,' I tell him. 'When I log into yourgoat.com, I get congratulated on winning prizes, I get loan offers, gaming sites, adverts for every conceivable item of lingerie and even paedophile grooming sites. In fact, particularly paedophile grooming sites. You close one down and the screen splits and up come another four. It's hopeless. The only way round it I have found is to turn it off and not bother.'

'Oh! I just put a hammer through the screen on mine,' said Jack.

'Anyway apart from that, Jack, I think that I've split, or multiplied,' I confide.

I can tell that Jack is surprised, although he is doing his best not to show it.

'I've just bought a new Saab,' he says.

In my dislocated state of mind, it is obvious that I am not going to get any work done. I tell Candice I am leaving for the day, ask her to take messages, and go to check my car. The bonnet is not too badly dented, a mere scratch really. I start the engine. The impact of the badger seems to have turned off the hazard lights and the radio has retuned itself to Radio 4. In case the other voice in my head starts up again I decide to drive home by way of the scenic route, taking me along Tambourine Road and Harmonica Way, a detour that I sometimes use when I need to unwind. There is hardly a murmur of traffic and only a small proportion of the cars are lilac. The air is still and evening seems to be descending even though it was mid-afternoon. On the radio, they are discussing Surrealism. This is oddly relaxing. Phrases like 'the disinterested play of thought,' and 'the omnipotence of the dream' float over me as I drive along. There is so much mental chewing gum on the radio. It is refreshing to hear an intellectual debate. The merits of Magritte, Miro and Dali are discussed in terms of their 'disdain for the thesis.' I have visited a few galleries recently and have been awestricken by some of the Surrealist works on show, so I can relate to much of what the art aficionados are saying. I am driving alongside the river. I stop, feeling it would be therapeutic to listen to the rest of the programme with the window wound down watching the river flow. The programme ends and I get out and sit on the riverbank.

As if I don't have enough to occupy my mind; no sooner has Jack left – in his new Saab – than he phones. 'Hi,' he says 'It's Jack.' My immediate thought is that he must have left something behind. 'I'm just dropping some woodwind instruments off in Scorcese Street, round the corner from you.' Jack sells musical instruments. 'I thought I might pop round for a cuppa afterwards if you're in. Be nice to have a chat.' I look at the clock. It is 11.22. 'OK s,see…. you in a bit,' I stammer.

While I might be able to appreciate modern art movements, I am old fashioned when it comes to temporal matters. I am comfortable with the idea of time moving forwards in a logical progression, numbers ascending as I was taught at school. Until midday. And then starting again. I like novels to have a linear narrative and get confused when the plot of a movie is told in flashbacks. The film, 'Memento' was to me, incomprehensible.

I try to take stock of the situation as I put some more cats out. Not only have I split – or multiplied – but I have regressed. Time is going backwards. I switch the TV on to Discovery 3 to see how their scheduling is matching up. A programme on Renaissance Art is just finishing. 'We continue,' says the presenter dressed in a crimson suit,' with our exploration of English Landscape Gardens, and at 12.30, we have a new series called 'Waterfalls.'

After a short while, I wander along the riverbank to 'The Black Hole' public house. The pub is not facetiously named: a Nobel Prize-winning quantum physicist lives nearby. No-one is sitting in the garden and the pub is almost empty. I order a half of Old Growler, take a sip and leave it on the bar while I go to the toilet. I wash my hands and look in the mirror. To my horror, I have no reflection. It would be easy to say I turned a whiter shade of pale, but there was no way of confirming this. I frantically check the mirror to see if it is some kind of trick device. It isn't. I feel the panic rising.

I leave my drink and practically run out of the pub. Outside it is very still and eerily quiet. There seems to be no background noise at all. I drop the proverbial pin. I look around me anxiously. The river has stopped flowing. The ripples on the water do not change. Ducks and gulls sit motionless on the surface. Boats move neither upstream nor downstream. A pair of swans are suspended in flight a few inches above the water. It is as if the riverscape had been captured in a painting. I stand dumbfounded for what might be a few minutes, but time seems to have lost some of its meaning. Suddenly, from out of nowhere a large group of sweating cyclists in a rainbow of pulsating colour comes hurtling down the road. The river starts up again and the air is full of birds, all eager to express their avian attributes with squawks and shrills. I go to check to see if my reflection has returned in the wing mirror of the car.

Jack's visit is very bizarre because I know in advance everything that he is going to say, and everything that I am going to say too. I find myself laughing a little ahead of his putting the hammer through his computer screen, but otherwise, the time passes without event. Eventually, he leaves – in his Saab.

Cable TV has a wealth of attractions. It is not all tacky game shows and repeats of British sitcoms from the 1970s. Amongst the irredeemable pap, there are channels devoted to programmes you just wouldn't find on terrestrial TV. So it is that I find 'String Theory and You' on Science and Technology channel.

It seems that the universe is shaped like a thin membrane, surrounded by higher dimensions that transcends the familiar dimensions of height, width and depth. Other universes are stacked alongside it. The membrane universe repeatedly folds over on itself, resulting in multiple universes adjacent to each other.

Inasmuch as time and space would be arbitrary, String Theory appears to be ideal in explaining how there were two of me, or how I can be in two places at once, living two separate lives in parallel universes very close to one another. Coincidences occur where two universes touch. Parallel lives are the result of a small fissure at this point. I am a little comforted by this explanation as I get the car out for the school run, and sit watching the river flow, simultaneously.

My car is painted primrose. As there is a small hole in the membrane of my universe and I have slipped through, all the other cars on the street are painted primrose too. Fortunately, there are no arachnids in the car but it is still difficult to concentrate. I am glad that it is only a short drive to Jessica's school.

# Benito and Tiffany

Tiffany Golden possesses a rare talent. She knows that things are going to happen before they do. As a result of her premonitory powers, Tiffany's life has been alternately comforting or frightening, depending on what is scheduled to happen. Unfortunately knowing that something is going to occur does not give Tiffany powers to prevent the eventuality. Try as she might, to take steps to avoid something unpleasant, she has not found a means to do so. She has however developed her persuasive powers to prevent too much disappointment or distress. Sometimes destiny needs a helping hand.

Tiffany Golden is not a clairvoyant or fortune teller. She cannot tell which horse is going to win the Derby, or if there is going to be an earthquake. She only knows what is going to happen in relation to her. If she were to put a bet on a horse, she would know if she was going to pick up money later on, and if the earthquake was going to affect her daily life, then she would know about it, otherwise she has the same faculties as those without the gift.

Today, the first Friday in April, her day will be alternately tiresome and exciting. Tiresome that she knows she is going to be waiting for twenty minutes in the tailback on the Buena Vista bypass, exciting that she knows she is going to meet Benito Van Horn in the tropical fish department of the pet superstore on the retail park at three o'clock, even though she never goes there and has no interest in tropical fish. She knows with equal certainty that, although he is a complete stranger, with just a fleeting glance in her direction, Benito will make her heart skip a beat. In short she knows that Benito Van Horn will sweep her off her feet.

Benito Van Horn does not possess such a talent. Dashing and debonair he might be in his dark blue suit, but he comes across as preoccupied. He has been told he can be unaccommodating and unresponsive. Casual and dispassionate are also terms that have been thrown at him. In the studio where he works as a producer, musicians that he is recording say that he is oblivious to how they would like to play. He takes the edge out of their music. Whatever they play he makes it sound like the famously bland band, *Keane*.

Benito is often not aware that something has happened even after it has. It was not until his decree absolute arrived on the mat that he realised his wife, Ursula had started divorce proceedings. He had thought that she was on holiday with her friend, Sharita. Try as he might Benito has found himself unable to redress his shortcomings. An army of life coaches, psychologists and consultants have become exasperated at his inability to change. They all say his aloofness is astonishing. If only they had the time, he could be a textbook study for a new condition.

It is three o'clock now on the first Friday in April and Benito Van Horn has absolutely no idea that he is glancing in Tiffany Golden's direction, let alone that his glance is making a lasting impression on her. In fact, so unobservant is he that he has not even grasped that he is in the tropical fish department in the pet superstore. He has only stepped in there to buy a house rabbit for his sister in law, Mercedes, who will be nineteen on Sunday.

Tiffany Golden leaves the pet superstore with a warm glow, brought about by Benito's loving gaze. She understands that he has been too shy to approach her, but she knows this is not going to matter. She sits in her yellow *Mini Cooper* with the black stripes and waits for Benito to leave and get in his own car. She knows this is a black *Toyota Auris* with a 64 plate. She knows that she is going to follow him home, even though she already knows where he lives. She knows that within a week she is going to be spending nights there.

Benito's awareness of fate is non-existent. When, having stalked him for days, Tiffany calls round to his house, he still does not recognise her.

'Are you the *Avon* lady?' he asks. 'I'm afraid that Ursula has gone away.'

He is surprised by the kiss. It is not the type of apologetic peck on the cheek you might expect from someone selling beauty products door to door, who has accidentally called at the wrong house. It is a passionate take your breath away all out assault on his face. It is the type of kiss you might expect from an aroused lover. It is the type of kiss that in a raunchy film might serve as a prelude to the participants ripping off each others' clothes. Having established that she is not the *Avon* lady and finding that things are happening down below, Benito responds with wild abandon. He is not at all sure what is happening or if what is happening is happening to him. But despite this uncertainty, in no time at all they are upstairs and are indeed ripping off one another's clothes. A little later, after a bout of bountiful coupling, he asks her name.

'Tiffany Golden,' she says.

'Well, Tiffany Golden,' says Benito Van Horn. 'That was ….. unexpected. I don't know what came over me. I'm not usually so …… forward,'

'I do hope that isn't so,' says Tiffany. 'I was hoping we might do it again soon.'

'I think that it was possibly the most unusual …. experience of my life,' says Benito.

'I knew that this was going to happen, so there was no point in fighting it,' says Tiffany Golden.

'I couldn't help but notice that you weren't fighting it,' says Benito. 'I'm Benito Van Horn by the way,'

'I know,' says Tiffany.'

'You do?'

'I think I probably know everything about you.'

It is the third Thursday in May. Tiffany Golden is now living with Benito Van Horn. As long as she takes the lead, she gets what she wants. She is happy with this arrangement. She has shown photos of Benito to her friends and her colleagues at the advertising agency, and they all think that he is a dreamboat. It is disconcerting that Benito doesn't always notice that she is there, but there are small signs that he might be changing. Once or twice lately he has greeted her with kisses when she has got back from work. As she drives home from the office along the Santa Rosa Boulevard, she wonders if today is going to be one of those days. This is an odd sensation for Tiffany because she feels she should know definitely one way or the other. Perhaps Benito will not even be home. Maybe he will be mixing muzak at the studio, or perhaps it is his sister in law, Portia's birthday and he has had to take an animal round. Tiffany is not accustomed to such uncertainty. She is sure though that it will pass.

Benito has noticed that there are more house plants to water and the washing machine is nearly always on. The kitchen is filling up with cookery books and kitchen utensils that he does not know the names of. The red wine has been replaced with white. Pink paperbacks with titles in handwritten script and cover illustrations of smiling young women in white chiffon are appearing on the bookshelf. There is no longer room in the wardrobe for all of his dark blue suits. There is a chess game going on with the bottles in the bathroom. He has noticed that Tiffany is around the place more than she used to be, in fact nearly all the time. Did she ask if she could move in? Did he say she could? Should he ask her if she asked him when she gets home from work?

Benito finds it a little worrying that Tiffany tends to be right all of the time, but on balance, he enjoys her company. Tiffany wears raunchier lingerie that Ursula did, laughs heartily at his badly told jokes, and is unexpectedly good at solving those tricky popular culture allusion clues to finish the Guardian cryptic crossword on a Saturday. And he likes the way she sometimes surprises him in the shower. He wonders if he ought to clear some of his old equipment out of the garage to make room for Tiffany's *Pro Trainer All In One Gym* and maybe paint over the grey in the spare room with a brighter colour. Blue perhaps.

Benito starts to prepare the ingredients for an omelette. He will remember to put the peppers and mushrooms in this time. The one last Thursday was a little bland without them.

'Anyone home,' choruses Tiffany. She knows that Benito is home because the Toyota is parked in its usual way across both parking spaces on the drive. The music that is playing, while it still has a discernible melody, has traces of dubstep and acid jazz. It is a departure from the bland overproduced middle of the road music she is used to him playing while she is out of the house. 'I like the music. What is it?'

'Oh, that's one I made earlier, says Benito. 'While you were at the hairdressers.'

'I haven't been to the hairdressers. I've been working,' says Tiffany.

'Oh, that's right,' says Benito. 'While you were at the travel agents.'

'Ad agency,' says Tiffany. 'I work at AdAge. It's an ad agency. Remember, you picked me up from there. You remarked on what a clever play on words it was.' She is secretly pleased that although one or two things seem to have changed lately, Benito still retains hints of his heedlessness. Detachment is part of his charm.

'I'm just making us an omelette,' he says. Afterwards, I thought we might go out to the greyhound racing. You keep telling me how much you like dogs.'

'Did I say that?' she says. Watching a bunch of skinny mutts chasing an electric rabbit round a gravel track has not been not on her radar. She was budgeting for a quiet night in with a bottle of Prosecco and a scented bath. Then perhaps Benito could give her a massage with the new oils she had bought. She hopes she is not witnessing a change in the dynamic of their relationship. With the dimming of her prescience, is Benito attempting to take over the decision making?

It is second Saturday in July. Tiffany Golden comes home from the hairdressers to the sound of Sufi music. Are there whirling dervishes in the front room, she wonders. Each day this week she has come home to increasingly unusual music. Each time she has asked Benito what it is, it has been 'something that he mixed that day'. On Monday it was garage punk, on Tuesday it was psytrance. On Wednesday it was psychedelic rock, on Thursday it was trip hop.

'What is it today?' asked Tiffany yesterday.

'Steampunk animé with a touch of drum and bass,' said Benito.

'The melody has all but disappeared,' said Tiffany.

Benito Van Horn, Tiffany realises, is changing. He doesn't even wear his dark blue suit anymore and he hardly ever shaves. And why does he wear sunglasses around the house? While she understands that two people in a relationship tend to mould each other to some degree, she is not sure that the changes are going in the right direction. She remembers making a casual comment a while back that they probably didn't get out enough but Benito seems insensitive to her interests. Over the past week, she has been treated to a twenty-twenty cricket match, a rugby sevens tournament, an orienteering workshop and a strip show. Although Benito claims they had discussions regarding plans for these evenings out, she has no recollections of these.

Accustomed to knowing in advance what is going to happen, each day now she is racked with anxiety about what is going to take place. Surely not another night at the dog track, or a rock climbing weekend. There were times in the past when she felt the burden of knowing what was going to happen was an irritation. It weighed heavily on her shoulders, but this was compensated by its comforts. Why is it she is no longer able to call the shots? Has she lost the gift of prescience completely?

Benito doesn't know what is wrong. Tiffany no longer wears raunchy lingerie and has stopped surprising him in the shower. He has even painted the spare room purple for her and put up some shelves to accommodate her growing selfhelp book collection. Surely it can't be his comment about her putting on weight. He had meant it in a nice way.

'I thought we might go to see some Sufi tonight, darling,' he says. 'So I put this sampler together to get us in the mood.'

Tiffany registers a robust look of disapproval. Benito thinks she is beginning to seem more like Ursula every day. He turns the music down a little.

'We can have a curry,' he says. '*Akbar's* has an excellent selection of Punjabi dishes and the cabaret comes on at nine. Authentic *qawwali* music.'

'I hate this awful wailing and I hate curry,' screams Tiffany. What could she have ever seen in Benito Van Horn? The man is singularly intolerable. How, she wonders had she not seen this situation coming?

'We could go to *Ping Pong* and have some noodle dishes if you prefer,' he continues, seemingly oblivious to his falling star. 'They have bamboo music, I believe, That's quite gentle.'

'I hate you,' she shrieks.

'Or we could just go *The Black Horse* for a pie and a game of darts, if you like.'

'You just don't get it, do you?'

'You'll be hungry later on.'

'I'm leaving you.'

It is the second Sunday in September. Tiffany Golden is pleased to be shot of Benito Van Horn. She is starting to enjoy life again. While her rare talent is still not fully functioning, she is beginning to get her premonitory powers back. Just last week, she foresaw that she was going to meet a tall stranger with blond curls who would sweep her off her feet. And here she is driving along Las Palomas in her new Mini Cooper S Coupé with the roof down to meet *DoubleTake*.

*DoubleTake's* singer, Ben Cool with his blond hair and black suede eyepatch is a dreamboat. *AdAge* has won the contract to handle the band's PR. Naturally, Tiffany has volunteered to take personal control of the contract. What she doesn't realise is that Benito Van Horn has died his hair blond and changed his name to Ben Cool. He didn't even realise he could sing, until about a month ago when he was recording the overdubs for *HashTag's* album, and now look at him. His fifteen minutes of fame beckons. What he doesn't know is that the agency his management company have hired to handle the band's promotion is *AdAge.*

# The Vexillographer's Daughter

## ONE: RAIN

It had rained every single day for the three summer months. Every morning at around five past seven with my bacon and egg sunny side up I would watch the weather forecast on *JustNews*. The weather presenter would come on and shrug sheepishly in front of a weather map of the UK covered in black clouds, and apologise for the synopsis he or she was about to offer. *JustNews* had attempted to break up the monotony a little by promising different intensities of rain from day to day, thunderstorms, heavy downpours, incessant rain, squally showers, patchy rain, or plain old ordinary persistent drizzle, these blamed on a variety of distinctive and often unexpected frontal systems pushing in from the Atlantic, coming in off the North Sea or crossing the channel. *Risk of flash flooding* was a phrase frequently used along with 'you'll need to take your umbrella'. *JustNews* had tried their best not to be completely downbeat or discouraging and only once or twice suggested we might be experiencing monsoons. Even then they had been careful to add that what we could expect was nothing compared to Bangla Desh or Pakistan where they were suffering the real thing, rivers forty miles wide, tens of millions of displaced people and all of that. They had never once gone so far as to argue that weather patterns for the UK had changed and rain and more rain was what we could anticipate for the foreseeable future. Occasionally there had been a cheery grinning face in front of a map showing lots of sun graphics and temperatures in the high 20s, but these never seemed to materialise.

They had even over the last few days, I couldn't help but notice, introduced the idea of shapely babes showing acres of leg and cleavage to stand in front of the sodden UK, but this had made little difference. However you dressed it up, it was going to rain. If it was not raining by the time I got in the car, it would be raining by the time I got to work. Admittedly it was a long commute from Oxford to Norwich which increased the chances of running into a shower or two, but most days the wipers on the Isuzu were running non-stop. Quite often the journey which should have taken just three hours in the powerful SUV took four or five, as I struggled to avoid roads that might be flooded.

Imogen and I had often talked about relocating closer to the flag design studio where I plied my trade. Huntingdon and Cambridge had been mentioned. But there never seemed to be the time to look into the idea, what with Imogen's beagle breeding business taking off and the time and energy taken up by Kurt's seemingly endless run of court appearances. There hadn't been any reported fires in the area for a while now so hopefully Kurt had at least grown out of his arson fascination, although it would be hard to describe his behaviour as exemplary. It would be fair to say that on the whole things at home were less fraught since Ann had gone off on her gap year. She seemed to view 42 Auden Avenue as a twenty four hour hotel. Now at least there was only one teenager in the house and one source of dissonant music. Ann and her friend, Drew, who was a few years her senior, had set off on a round the world trip, quite suddenly I felt, at the end of June. We had, of course, rowed about it, with me pretending to be completely against the idea, but I had to admit she would in all probability learn a lot more about life than she would have at Warwick or Winchester. I only wished that I had had the imagination to have done the same at her age. And as Imogen had pointed out Ann had always been a bit of a tomboy. Not being at home as much I did not notice these things, but she did play a lot of rugby. Drew, if Kurt was to be believed was a lesbian, or a 'rug muncher' as he so delicately put it. 'She's got a man's name innit,' he had offered by way of explanation. 'And she's got a kd lang haircut.' This was lost on me as I had no idea who kd lang was. I did not give the idea much credence. Kurt was always coming up with wild stories. Ann's hair seemed perfectly normal for someone of her age, long and short, up and down, straight or wavy and a different colour every week. She never tidied her room, left clothes scattered around the house, CDs out of their cases, and copies of Curve and Diva magazines lying around just as you would expect. I took Ann and Drew to Heathrow and there was no sign of any funny business. On the journey, we talked about the national characteristics of different countries and of course flags and the many of the other things that come up in everyday conversation. I helped them with their suitcases and I slipped Ann an envelope with a couple of hundred pounds in it while we had a cappuccino in the departure lounge. 'Keep in touch,' I said - and we had had a postcard or two from India, weather very hot, cows on the streets and lots of beggars, that sort of thing. The last we had heard from Ann, they were in Kyoto valeting *love hotels* to pay for their flight to Darwin.

Family life was pretty much on the back burner as I was very busy working on the commissions that had come my way over the last few weeks to design flags for three breakaway Russian republics and an up and coming African state. The extra work had kept me in Norwich sometimes late into the night and once or twice I had stopped over. Imogen, remarking that I never seemed to be around to help her rotovate the vegetable garden, or clear out the loft, or make sure Kurt kept his appointments with the Youth Offending team, had a few times in desperation suggested that I might be able to design flags somewhere nearer to home.

'What exactly do you do?' and 'How difficult can it be to draw a few lines and colour them in?' were typical remarks showing her lack of appreciation of the complexities of designing flags. Also, she did not seem to understand that Norwich was the established flag design centre in the UK, perhaps even Europe. If you wanted to be in the vanguard of vexillography Norwich was the only place to be.

## TWO: BIG COUNTRY

Is Australia ever big? I hadn't realised just how staggeringly huge Australia is. When you see it in the bottom right-hand corner of the map it looks like an afterthought. But, trust me, it is colossal. The Stuart Highway running from Darwin to the south of the continent, Drew and I noticed from The Rough Guide, runs for 2,834 kilometres. The road signs we passed in the Toyota coming out of Darwin displayed absurd distances such as Adelaide 3,034 kilometres and Sydney 4,084. I don't think we really believed we were going to complete such a journey; we were just going to go with the flow and see what happened. No point in making plans; this was an , not a commitment. Perhaps we would get to Alice Springs, where we might be able to get the odd days work in a bar or restaurant. We'd seen some awesome blogs about Alice Springs. Or Brisbane. Brisbane sounded cool. Plenty of Brits in Brisbane, the Guide said. And Fortitude Valley, wherever that was, was wicked, we'd been told. We were, of course, travelling on a budget and the beaten up old Toyota which we hired from *Bazza's Car Hire* in Darwin had no air conditioning or sunroof, no radio, no speedometer and no headlights. And an oil indicator light that stayed on. Whether it was down to Drew driving with the handbrake on or me not being able to change up from third, the engine kept overheating. We were both crap drivers. Drew had failed her driving test five times back home. And I did not have a licence at all, but Bazza hadn't worried too much about that. He just wanted to look at our legs and maybe get the scruffy old wreck off the lot. It didn't seem to matter therefore when we had a bit of a random shunt and lost the front bumper as the Toyota was so janky to begin with. You get what you pay for, Dad always used to say to me whenever my cheap phone or mp3 player broke, and we had paid diddly squat.

It was blisteringly hot and uncomfortably humid. Drew and I stripped down to shorts and bikini tops and even so these stuck to us like a second skin. The six five litre bottles of water we had bought at *Strewth Bruce* in Darwin were soon gone as we used it to pour over ourselves to cool down. We had to keep stopping for more. We had found India pretty warm but even the heat in Kolkata was nothing compared to this. Every twenty clicks inland we travelled, the temperature rose by one degree Celsius. By the time we got to Pine Creek the temperature had risen to over forty degrees. This was where the Toyota's engine finally blew up and we abandoned the smouldering heap by the side of the road. To lighten the load and lessen the panic of being stranded we started on the Darwin Stubbies we had in our bags. Warm beer but still very welcome.

'No sign of the Amber Nectar round here,' I said.

'I guess they don't drink it in Australia,' said Drew.

'Perhaps they wear cork hats either.'

'Or play cricket.'

'It's not the same country as the one on the posters back home is it?'

# THREE: FLAG

It was a Monday morning and I had been on the road for the best part of four hours driving through torrential rain. Honey, showing even more leg than Jasmine had the day before, had forecast 'isolated showers'. I was making very slow progress due to surface water on all of the roads from Oxford to East Anglia. I was listening to a Radio 4 discussion about why the country's largest supermarket chain had suddenly collapsed. This had replaced Hurricane Nigel as the number one news item. I was stuck in a long queue of traffic waiting on the approach to the Kings Lynn roundabout when I got an unexpected call on the handsfree. The world of flag design certainly has its share of spills and thrills, but I had never expected to get a call from the Prime Minister. He wanted me to redesign the British flag. With the prolonged bad weather, the run on the pound, the conflict in the Middle East, and what he termed a series of negative news items lately, he felt that confidence in the government and the country was at an all-time low. Then, of course, there had been the embarrassing performance in the football World Cup (who could forget the sending off of the entire English team) and the humiliation in the Test Series (in the matches that had not been rained off). People, he said, needed to see the nation in a new light and one of the key steps to redefining Britain was to come up with a new flag. The Union Jack comprising of St George's Cross, St Andrew's Cross and St Patrick's Cross as I well knew dated back to 1801, and a version without St Patrick's Cross dated back to 1606. Apart from its militaristic and racial subtexts the flag was to put it in a word, hopelessly old-fashioned both by design and as a symbol. The British people could no longer be fooled into thinking they ruled the waves. 'So we're going to ah, waive the rules.' The PM laughed nervously at his play on words.

During our conversation, which saw me edge ever nearer to the Kings Lynn roundabout, he confided that his radical cultural shake up plans also included a new National Anthem which he had given over to *Radiohead*, and moving Parliament to somewhere more contemporary, and indeed, higher up. I took it that he was referring to the fact that the present location as it was on the Thames might become flooded should the Thames Barrier be breached. Why was I based in Norwich, he was curious to know, and not somewhere more urbane and higher up?

He said he would call me again in a week and hung up just as I was coming off the roundabout. The rain seemed to have eased a little now leaving a free run to Norwich. I put on a relaxing CD of Boccherini string quartets and tried out the steering wheel isometrics that I had learned to release some of the tension that had accumulated from the long drive. As the big Isuzu powered along the A47, I was able to give some thought to the new commission. Environmental issues were being talked about a lot, what with the Earth Summit coming up. How about a green flag? There weren't many flags that were primarily green.... Well, Pakistan and Saudi Arabia were mostly green. And Libya's flag was entirely green. Perhaps these were not the right examples. What about a pink flag? I wondered. There were I could quite categorically say no pink state flags. Militaristic subtexts were not an issue with shocking pink, Pantone Process Magenta.

I should explain that flag design departs considerably from logo design: logos are predominantly still images to be read off a page, screen, or billboard. I occasionally dabbled in logo design. I had recently for instance designed the official *Recession* logo for the BBC, but on the whole, I steered clear of this enterprise. In a word logos are flat. Flags, on the other hand, are alternately draped and fluttering images to be seen from a variety of distances and angles. The prevalence of simple bold colours and shapes in flag design is paramount. It is customary to use primary colours and white or black. One of my personal favourite state flags is the Seychelles flag which is a bold geometric design consisting of four triangular shapes of blue: Pantone 294 yellow: Pantone 122 red: Pantone 1795 green: Pantone 356, each starting from the bottom left of the flag and sweeping out towards the top right. Ann had sent us a postcard of the Seychelles flag earlier in the year when she was working in a Surf Shop on Mahe Island to save up the money for her passage to India. They were planning to go to on to Japan and Australia, she had written matter of factly as if all these places were nearby.

# FOUR: BOOMERANG

We continued our trek south, hitching lifts with a succession of lecherous truck drivers with bad breath and crusty cattle farmers moving their stock. Our progress was slow. Although it was oppressively hot and we were minging, we made serious attempts to cover ourselves up. Some of these guys in the outback were really creepy. Mikey, a bauxite mining engineer from Wagga Wagga, who picked us up in his Mitsubishi 'ute; near Emu Hole had a Bobby Peru grin and the seduction technique of a bull seal. He was revolting. He had a smile like an alligator. He talked on his CB radio to someone called *Jeck* about how he was bringing two dirty little *beaches* over and how they would be able to 'fuck them like jeck rebbit bunnies'. 'You bitter deegout year rittlesneke Jeck, we'll be thayer in foive.' Perhaps I've got the accent wrong but while he was still talking his strine bogan jive, he grabbed be by the neck and pulled me towards him. I screamed and Drew using her ample bulk dived in to help. In the frantic struggle that followed the Mitsubishi left the road, but Mikey had locked the doors so we couldn't get out.

It was fortunate that Koorong, a hunky native didgeridoo maker from Timber Creek, came along at this moment in an old flatbed truck which was loaded with brightly painted instruments. Not so lucky though that he was headed west. Although we were grateful to have been rescued, this was one of a run of rides that took us hundreds of clicks off course. We would have preferred to carry on by the most direct route down *the track*, as the vast Stuart Highway was commonly known, but we were taken along a selection of single lane roads and rough tracks on a zigzag through the Northern Territory. Koorong seemed to be in no hurry. He chewed hallucinogenic plants and talked to us about Walkabout and Dreamtime. In the time before Time, he told us, there was only the barren land and the empty sky. The sun, moon and stars slept below the land along with the spirits. On the First Day, the Sun was born from the land. He rose into the sky and his light warmed the land. Slowly the other Ancestors awoke and emerged onto the land. This marked the beginning of the Dreamtime. As the Ancestors crossed the land they spoke names, calling into being all of creation, natural features as well as plants and animals and even abstract concepts such as death. They sang songs which incorporated the names they had created. They left a web of songlines on the land which indicated their progress. During their travels, the Ancestors also deposited guruwari particles, the seeds of life which have existed through the generations and through these particles life today is linked with life in the Dreamtime.

'This place belongs to my ancestors,' he continued. 'It is our spirit. We, the aboriginal people live in this country as one spirit. But today because of the white man's consumption and greed, the ancestral way is threatened by climate change. We are always looking at the seasons. The dry season is now very hot. You will see if you stay here. And what water there is can be bad. The food cycles are shifting. We need to get back to the Dreaming to ensure the continuity of life and the land.'

Having been brought up with a different story, Drew and I were grateful for this fascinating explanation of creation and were saddened by what we in the twenty first century were doing to Koorong's heritage.

The slowness of these days in the outback gave me time to reflect. I had escaped the two crazy lunatics I had spent my life living with. Can you imagine, Dad made me collect stamps. Every week, until I was about sixteen, he would march me down to the philatelists (yes they do still exist) to buy a set from Paraguay, Vietnam or the Dutch East Indies or similar far off places, and supervise me at home while I stuck them in my album. He was completely obsessed. Quite anal about the whole exercise. Don't you think you should put the Johore ones into the India pages? I remember him saying. Some of the stamps were quite rare. I had a set from Qatar with pictures of the first Soviet astronauts that was worth several thousand pounds. I did have some pretty ones with butterflies on from Tristan da Cunha that were valuable and a Silver Jubilee set from Basutoland. I hadn't let on to Dad that I had sold these on the internet to buy my iphone. He was not very observant. When I had my hair cut short and died purple a year or so back, he did not notice. He did not ever comment on the fact that I never brought boys home or that Drew stayed over quite a lot. He also did not seem to be aware of what the rainbow bracelets and earrings I wore signified. He was in his own world. He had this annoying habit of whistling Elton John or Dave Brubeck tunes when he was in the house. I didn't mind the Elton John so much, but can you imagine anyone trying to whistle *Blue Rondo a La Turk*? Admittedly it was a big house but it was hard to get way from Dad's collections of Coronation memorabilia, pre-war cameras, licence plates, Macintosh computers and of course, flags. Perhaps everyone thinks of their parents embarrassing but if Dad was mad and a little remote, Mum was barking. She would dress up her dogs and take them to shows, no not dog shows, she would take them to *Mamma Mia* and *Les Miserables*. Totally kooky! I was only now able to appreciate that I was finally free from all that. Oz was, by comparison, sane.

Koorong introduced us to ostrich eggs which were I would have to say a bit tastier than some of the other fare on offer. He lived it seemed mainly on a diet of bandicoot, tubers and insects. He showed us how to make a fire by rubbing sticks together and to my surprise after a few attempts I found this remarkable easy. But pointless as I always carried a lighter. He showed us how to craft a didgeridoo from a eucalyptus branch and how to throw a left-handed boomerang (like we needed to know). Despite our Rough Guide, we really had no idea at any moment where we were or where we were going. This was off the map. The alien flora and fauna and the strange indigenous wildlife that we saw around us made it seem like another planet. We saw red kangaroos, water buffalos and packs of fierce looking dingoes. We saw scary lizards of all shapes and sizes and colossal birds of prey swooping on the roadkill in the open areas. We were treated to spine-chilling stories of venomous snakes slithering in beside people in their beds. Tales of bloodsucking bugs and spiders the size of a volleyball. We saw nine foot tall Aboriginals, tree-climbing crocodiles and two-headed dragons. The hallucinatory landscape of the *Top End* as the northern half of Australia was known both entranced and terrified us.

'Just think,' said Drew one night. 'You could be at uni in Reading reading Renaissance texts and the Romantic poets. Wouldn't you rather be doing that?'

'And you could be coordinating conferences in Cowley,' I said, sliding my hand between her legs.

I think we both knew where we wanted to be.

# FIVE: FLOOD

When I arrived at the office there was a message from Imogen. I could hear the nerve jangling chords of *Dying Fetus* or *Angel Corpse* playing in the background, which meant that Kurt was at home, something unlikely to have improved Imogen's disposition. I spent the rest of the day running through her list of grievances, chasing up the cowboy contractors who were supposed to be fitting the air conditioning for the new kennels and the plant hire company who claimed that the rotavator we had hired was overdue. We had returned it last month, along with the stump grinder. I wrangled with the internet service provider over the broadband contract and tried to negotiate with the vicar over the damage to the church that he alleged Kurt and his friends had been responsible for. Later in the day another band of torrential rain blew over from the west and set in and I found myself stranded in Norwich on account of the floods. Norfolk and Cambridgeshire, traditionally two of the driest areas of the country, were particularly badly hit. Most of the rivers in both counties had burst their banks. I asked Rachel to find a hotel. Rachel always seemed to know which hotel to book. Also, where the best restaurants were.

The following day as I worked on some initial designs on my Mac with Radio 4 in the background, the news was pretty grim. Inflation had hit a twenty year high and the stock market was in turmoil. All of the major money markets had taken a tumble but the FTSE was in free-fall. One of the UK's largest and most revered financial institutions had collapsed, the one we had our mortgage with as it happened, and the Youth Offending Service called to say that Kurt had missed his appointment. Late in the afternoon the PM rang to see how I was getting on with the flag. His voice echoed the pressure he was clearly under. He sounded desperate.

'I need it by Friday,' he said.

I told him I was working on some ideas and that Friday wouldn't be a problem.

'You won't let me down, Paul, will you?' he pleaded.

I called an emergency meeting of my team for a brainstorming session. Flag design isn't labour intensive and my team wasn't a large team. It consisted of just myself, Rachel and Magda, the work experience placement who came in to service the Linotype and maintain the roof garden.

The flag did need to be a departure. Rules as I saw it were there to be broken. Perhaps there were no rules, only perceived limitations.

'Think radical,' I told the others. 'Think outside the box. leftfield' I couldn't believe I was coming out with these clichés, the banal staples of business meetings, conference calls and lengthy self-indulgent speeches. Could anything be considered radical or leftfield in this postmodern digital age which emphasises the elusiveness of meaning and knowledge? There were, after all, no overarching truths anymore. Narratives were all tainted by the concept of the unreliable author. Now everyone could be famous for fifteen minutes.

Rachel took up the challenge. 'Damien Hirst did a series of paintings of dozens of different coloured spots, a bit like a colour chart.'

I felt that the idea was a tad hackneyed. I had recently seen a similar design on Imogen's mother's ironing board cover. The perception of an art flag, a flag that made a statement as a work of art was an appealing one though especially if you delved a little deeper into the history of art. The 1960s geometry of Frank Stella or Gene Davis, to which it could be argued Damien Hirst's paintings owed a debt, would suit a flag. I made a note.

'What about a white flag,' suggested Magda. 'For peace.'

'A white flag means surrender,' I pointed out. 'Universally.' But I couldn't argue that the idea was not 'outside the box'.

'A black flag'

'A transparent flag'

'A mirror flag'

'An invisible flag'

'A virtual flag'

The ideas kept coming. Magda was clearly on a roll. Perhaps I was not making the best use of her skills getting her to plant santolinas, bronze fennel and Iceland poppies up there on the roof.

My mobile rang. It was Imogen. She sounded distraught - and confrontational. Bella, one of her favourite beagles had been savaged by a Staffordshire bull terrier, an alarmingly ugly brute with fangs like a tyrannosaurus rex. She had rushed Bella to Village Vets where she was now in the Emergency Room with Dr Marciano fighting to save her life. I tried my best to console Imogen but it seemed the call had been primarily to apportion blame. We managed during the heated exchange that followed to establish that it was my fault for not getting round to repairing the fence. My excuse that it had been too wet lately did nothing to improve my standpoint and we ended the conversation without the usual pleasantries.

No sooner had I put the phone down than Kurt phoned asking if he could borrow a *ton*. Sensing my reluctance, he added, 'I could always find it another way, you get me.'

'What is it for?' I asked, hoping he might surprise me with something like, 'it's to buy the new digital Encyclopaedia Brittanica' or 'to buy some new weatherproofs for the geography field trip.' His thinly veiled threat, 'Or I could tell mum what you're really up to in Norwich' suggested he was not going to tell me what it was for, so it was probably for drugs. Admittedly he was nearly fifteen but a hundred pounds did seem to be quite a large sum for a personal amount of cannabis. It seemed however that I was on a loser to nothing by pursuing the matter. I told him where I kept the float for emergency household situations.

'I already know that innit?' he said with a laugh. 'I was just being polite like. SYL.' He was even talking in text now.

I momentarily contemplated the discrepancy between my global influence and my domestic authority. I had the trust of the Prime Minister and other heads of state but my own family saw me as a doormat. Perhaps everything in life had a tendency to balance out. Yin-yang according to Mi Fu, my traditional acupuncturist, is a dynamic equilibrium. Because the two opposites arise together they are always equal: if one disappears, the other must disappear as well, leaving emptiness. This I was told is rarely immediately apparent because yang elements are clear and obvious while yin elements are hidden and subtle. I had heard on a science programme on the radio the other day that a chunk of Canada the size of Scotland had broken off and was heading south. Sea levels were expected to rise significantly as the ice melted. The next item had been about how mathematicians had discovered a new prime number with 1,300 digits. So it goes. Tomorrow there might be a dozen more flood alerts but Natasha might read the weather in Agent Provocateur lingerie.

After a good deal of deliberation over a bottle or two of New World red, we settled on a vibrant flag design based on a contemporary Aboriginal art postcard that Ann had sent, a startling riot of colour that we felt would stand out anywhere. It was so vivid you might need special sun specs to view it. This was the breakthrough that we had been waiting for, the design that would put *Paul Caruso Flags* well and truly on the map. Once the new British standard was raised, leaders of nations would be queuing up with their commissions for new flags.

Our optimistic representations did nothing to temper the inclement weather. The wind turned round to the north gathering in strength, and heavy showers persisted through the afternoon. Rachel and I once again found ourselves stranded and were forced to stay another night in the *Georgian House Hotel*. The following morning the biggest bank in the country collapsed, the one I had my savings with as it happened, the FTSE hit a twenty year low, and Imogen phoned to say that Kurt had bought an air rifle and was firing at the fantail doves in the Henderson-Gough's garden. At least she thought it was an air rifle. It was certainly a gun of some sort. I was unable from the muffled report I heard in the background to confirm the type of weapon. I told her I would deal with it later, but for her not to call the police just yet. I was fairly sure that a hundred pounds would not have purchased an AK47 or anything like that. Imogen did not, however, seem happy with my uncooperative response and we picked up the stock conversation we employed for such disputes.

Around midday the storm surge generated by the low pressure all around the British Isles funnelled down the North Sea and at high tide the Thames barrier was breached. London began to flood. Within an hour the central districts along the river from Greenwich up to Chiswick were inundated. The underground network was closed and the rush to leave the city was causing gridlock on all roads. Rachel and I, still holed up in the hotel, watched the news as it happened on JustNews.

At 4pm, the Prime Minister phoned from Muswell Hill where Parliament had convened to a temporary location by Alexandra Palace. This he explained was 'ah, one of the highest places in London.'

I wondered where the highest place in East Anglia might be.

'The flag, Paul!' said the PM. 'Can we start producing some? The public need a distraction.'

I told him a little about the design and the process.

'I don't care about any of that,' he said. 'Just get it to me.'

I was about to put the phone down when he said, 'by the way, Paul. On a brighter note, you'll be pleased to know can now download Radiohead's new National Anthem off the Direct Gov website. I'm told by my musical advisor that it sounds, ah, cool. Have a listen and see what you think.'

## SIX: ALICE

When we finally made it back onto *the track*, The Magnetic Ant Hills dominated the landscape; these so called we were told by a crusty Norwegian backpacker with an unpronounceable name because they are orientated in a north-south direction, on account of the way the termites react to the position of the sun during the day, or something like that. And there was sun in abundance. Every minute of each day the sun burned down with unrelenting ferocity. There were no speed limits here, but no-one appeared to be in a hurry. We seemed to get rides that only took us a few clicks and then it would be hours before someone else stopped and one day passed into another. The distances on the signposts never seemed to get any smaller. We stayed sometimes in cheap run down backpackers hostels. One night we stayed in the shack where the owner, Wayne, a bogan redneck in flannelette shirt and stubbies, told us Frank Ifield wrote *She Taught Me How To Yodel*. Who? Another night we found ourselves under canvas at a Steve Irwin survival camp beneath the stars huddled together for warmth as the temperature dropped to around zero. How could this happen when it was so hot during the day? It is only then when you find yourself unable to sleep because of the unfamiliar nocturnal sounds that you realise that your tenure of this land is a fragile one. At any moment you feel you might be attacked by a giant porcupine, a forty foot ant or some other disgusting alien creature.

The further into the interior we went the drier it became. The drought-blighted hinterland was like an oven. No wonder there were so many bush fires in the outback. One match and there would be devastation across whole states. One discarded cigarette end could start the whole thing off. We passed through a place where it hadn't rained there for seven years. As we approached the Simpson Desert it was over fifty degrees. Only cacti grew here. It was four weeks since we had left Darwin and we were the colour of the natives, some of this may have been dirt and grime of course. There had been nowhere to take a decent shower since Darwin.

We finally made it back to something like civilisation. Places were closer together and we were able to get more frequent lifts. Little mining settlements gave way to bigger mining settlements and finally we reached Alice Springs at the end of November. I first became aware of the new British flag in Alice. Drew and I were in a bar sipping at a couple of cold *tinnies*. We had heard random stories from other trekkers in Alice and we were laughing about having avoided the floods back home, when lo and behold Dad appeared on the television that was playing in the corner of the bar. Struck dumb and rooted to the spot I was and the rest. It was a chat show on one of the hundreds of satellite channels that you can pick up even here in the outback. It was a British show; I recognised the presenter, although I could not think of his name. It was a noisy bar and the television was turned down so I did not catch much of the conversation but Dad was being talked up to as something of a celebrity. In between Dad holding forth, they kept focussing on a large Aboriginal painting. Drew and I had seen some like it in Darwin and one or two of the towns we had passed through. Hadn't I sent a postcard of something similar from Darwin? They showed a picture of what appeared to be the same painting flying as a flag above Buckingham Palace and I put two and two together. This must be a new British flag. What a weird design for a flag I thought, but it was probably no odder than the tie-dyed flag Dad had designed for the Federation of Balkan States. Thom Yorke of Radiohead was also a guest on the chat show and, although I did not grasp the connection there and then, the band performed what I later discovered was the new British National Anthem.

It was not until the following day when I saw the headline in The Alice Springs News that I realised that there was a controversy here in Australia over the new British flag because the existing Australian flag had in its left-hand top quarter the Union Jack. On the face of it you would not have thought that this was something the average Aussie would feel proud of or want to defend. You would have thought they would be glad to replace this symbol of colonial suppression with something a little closer to home. Not so. The Australian government it seemed were not at all keen to replace the Union Jack with an Aboriginal design. Giving Aboriginals voting rights was one thing, but acknowledging them on the national flag was altogether unacceptable. This was one step too far for a majority of white Australians. Further controversy arose from the fact that the Aborigines themselves were outraged that an Aboriginal design had been plundered by the super colonial power. The country was in uproar.

We kept an eye on the news sites on the net. Gradually the blame for the flag shifted from the British Prime Minister to the designer of the flag, largely I gathered through dad's unrelenting procession of chat show appearances. He probably even appeared on the one with the presenter that was always taking her kit off for *The Sun*, Tori something or other. He was shameless. I decided that I would not contact him.

Meanwhile, the name Caruso became reviled in Australia, and Australians took their hating very seriously. Zoo Weekly, the Australian magazine held an annual poll *Australia's Most Hated*. Near the top of the list the previous year in a mixed bag we found out were the Bali bomber, The Pope, and Toadie from Neighbours. The shows on television were inviting nominations for this year's poll and among the candidates being suggested was Paul Caruso. The knives were out.

Backpackers are constantly asked for identity in this over-bureaucratised country and Caruso was not a good name to have on your passport. We headed for Queensland, back into the bush. This joke might help to explain.

A Queensland farmer got in his truck and drove to a neighbouring farm and knocked at the farmhouse door. A young boy, about nine, opened the door.

'Is your Dad home'? the farmer asked.

'Sorry mate he isn't,' the boy replied. 'He went into town.'

'Well,' said the farmer, 'Is your Mum here'?

'No, mate, she's not here either. She went into town with Dad.'

'How about your brother, Greg? Is he here'?

'He went with Mum and Dad.'

The farmer stood there for a few minutes, shifting from one foot to the other and mumbling to himself.

'Is there anything I can do for ya'? the boy asked politely. 'I know where all the tools are if you want to borrow any, or maybe, I could take a message for Dad.'

'Well,' said the farmer uncomfortably, 'I really wanted to talk to your Dad. It's about your brother Greg getting my daughter pregnant.'

The boy considered for a moment.

'You'd have to talk to Dad about that,' he finally conceded. 'If it helps you any, I know that Dad charges $200 for the bull and $150 for the pig, but I really don't know how much he would be asking for Greg.'

Queensland you will gather is considered in Oz to be a tad rustic.

## SEVEN: CHAT

'You must be very pleased with the country's response to your new flag, Paul,' said Tori Kenyon, fiddling with her tortoiseshell glasses. I was. It had been well received at the opening of the new Parliament on Shooters Hill and at the Sports Personality of the Year ceremony, won for the second year running by that cyclist whose name escapes me. People were coming in their thousands from all over the world to see the flag flying majestically over Buckingham Palace, which had remarkably escaped the worst of the flooding. It had, I told Tori, been my proudest moment to been invited to the palace.

Radiohead's new National Anthem, by contrast, had had a mixed reception. Many had liked it but a number of people who were familiar with their oeuvre maintained that it was just an up-tempo remake of 'Fake Plastic Trees.' The Telegraph music critic took it a step further and suggested that 'civilisation as we know it is doomed and that brimstone is going to start raining from the sky any minute.'

'But a little concerned I'd imagine about its not going down so well down under?' continued Tori, fidgeting with the strap of the low cut top she was wearing. Tori was the new queen of chat show hosts on satellite TV, with a number of viewers' awards to her name. She had also appeared in various stages of undress in FHM and GQ, and had even I was told featured as a cover girl in Nuts. Kurt had probably jerked off over her.

I admitted that I was more than a little concerned as Tori put it about the colonials' reaction to the aboriginal design, not least because my daughter was out there.

'Yes. One or two of the tabloids picked up on this in the week didn't they?' smiled Tori. 'You haven't heard anything then?'

I told Tori that Ann's phone had been dead for a couple of weeks and that her last communication was an email sent ten days before from an unknown location. I had tried all the usual channels to try to find out where she might be. Unfortunately as part of the backlash against the threat to the Commonwealth Blue Ensign, the British Embassies in Canberra, Sydney, Brisbane, Melbourne and Perth were all under siege. There had been a number of supposed Ann sightings reported in the press but none of these had led to anything.

'She is probably on her way back home,' I said, 'but anyway if the tabloids can't track down an attractive twenty year old backpacker in Australia then I probably can't.' I realised as I said it that this did not come across as the attitude of a responsible parent. Now that I was a celebrity this would no doubt be picked up by the more moralising tabloids.

'And there was that little piece about your son Kurt being involved in Nazi style initiation ceremonies at his school,' continued Tori.

How had she found out about this? The article had only appeared in the Oxford local paper and they had not mentioned Kurt's name because he was a minor.

Before I had chance to comment she moved on to the affair that I was allegedly having and the impending divorce. We seemed to have lost sight of the subject that I was on the show to talk about, the celebration of the flag. I considered removing the microphone and walking off.

Tori seemed to sense that she had perhaps overstepped the mark and in an attempt to get me back on board she uncrossed her legs offering me a glimpse of her white panties.

'But of course on the positive side rumour has it that you have been invited to appear on *Celebrity Russian Roulette* on *Happy TV*,' she beamed. 'Not tempted by the generous cash prizes?'

'I don't think that I will be accepting the offer after what happened to Teddy Trimmer the darts player,' I replied. Teddy had been the first celebrity on the show to select the live chamber.

'You don't think that *Celebrity Russian Roulette* is stage managed then?' said Tori, looking up to see if her next guest was ready. The next guest I notice was the winner of *Celebrity Kidney Swap*. The concentration span of viewers of Tori's show was clearly mercilessly short.

'Not worth taking that chance, is it,' I said, but Tori was already introducing the short balding magician.

The short balding magician shook my hand as he passed and said, 'Good luck finding your daughter mate, I expect progress is slow because the Australian Police have their work cut out trying to find the people who are starting those terrible bush fires that we are hearing about on the news.'

It occurred to me slowly as I listened to Tori ask the short balding magician about the twilight of his career that Kurt may not, after all, have been the *Headington Firestarter*. There had been no reports of arson around Oxford since June. Perhaps Kurt was telling the truth for once. And Ann had always been the one who wanted to go to firework displays when she was younger.

## EIGHT: OUTBACK

Oh, my god! Dad thinks I may have started the forest fires that have been sweeping the south of the country. I spoke to Mum on the phone and I was horrified when she told me. What on earth is he on? What a shitbag! I'm never going to speak to him again. I can't believe he could think I would do such a thing. Just because Kurt got into a bit of trouble a while back. I don't even think it was Kurt that lit the fires in Headington. He was hanging round with those pikeys from the caravan site at the time. Elvis and Tyson and Danny. It is just that Kurt was stupid enough to take the blame.

All else aside, Drew and I haven't been anywhere near Victoria or New South Wales where the fires are. They're about two thousand kilometres away. Doesn't Dad know anything about geography? How big Australia is? I sent him an email three weeks ago now saying that we were in Richmond in Queensland and had got jobs on the Dinosaur Trail, thinking he would be pleased we were doing well - despite his best efforts to fuck things up for us with his throwaway comments on all those cheap chat shows back in the UK and his ridiculous tweets. He's really flipped. Mum's divorcing him. I don't blame her. How could she live with this obsessed crazy madman for so long? And all that crap he gave her about Norwich being the flag design capital when it was obvious he was having an affair there.

Anyway, the Dinosaur Trail is really cool. One hundred million years ago the Queensland outback lay under inland seas swarming with marine reptiles, and prehistoric creatures roamed the land. It has the most amazing fossils. It's in the middle of nowhere really and it's really laid back. No-one cares that we're Brits or who we are. Cannabis grows well in these parts and most of them are too stoned to notice.

We're totally incognito out here. It's brilliant. The Australian Parliament is still fighting over the flag, but again no one round here is bothered one way or another about politics. In the last election, Richmond had the lowest turnout anywhere in the country. And the weather's ace once you get used to the fact that for months on end it never rains.

# Thursday Night and Friday Morning

A car outside my window sounds its horn three times and I stir from my sleep. I was on a golden beach listening to the gentle echo of summer voices. Dolphins were playing with gondolas in the surf. A woman with long dark hair and iridescent tantric tattoos who I met on a balloon trip was rubbing oil into my back and talking in soft Italian. A man in a harlequin suit with a limp was selling doughnuts, and dwarf camels, as small as cats, were frolicking around pyramids that children had made in the sand.

I drift back off, but the disturbance outside has been enough to change the landscape of my dream. I am now in a crowded market-place and a hooded figure riding a jet black quad bike and waving a dead fish is chasing me past stalls selling large bongo drums and ritual masks. He is shouting at me in a language I do not recognise. I wonder if it is Welsh, but it may not be. I shout back in a language I do not recognise. It is dark and I trying to find my car. I cannot remember what make of car it is or where I have left it. I have the thought that it is not a Maserati or an Alfa Romeo, but this does not seem to help much. There is a large moon low in the sky and shapes of a craggy landscape are in silhouette. I am running. I have a battered leather suitcase in my hand. I have not packed it properly and Monica's clothes are spilling out onto the cobbled stone street. I make an effort to look back but I know the scene is disappearing. There is a faint light ahead, but this too is becoming fainter and more distant.

The horn outside sounds a piercing continuous note. I feel disorientated. My flailing arms meet with a sharp cry of feline disapproval and my bedside lamp crashes to the floor. It takes me a while to take in that it is Thursday night, or to be more precise 1 a.m. on Friday morning, and that the car outside is a taxi to take me out drinking. I had completely forgotten.

I do not mean that I have missed a rendezvous with friends. Or that I need a drink. I am not an alcoholic or anything like that; in fact, I only recently started drinking alcohol. And I am not by any means a night owl. Early to bed, early to rise, me.

I will try to explain. The new law obliges me to drink. Firstly the government passed licensing laws permitting round the clock drinking. They argued at the time that twenty-four hour opening for pubs and clubs would reduce binge drinking and help to tackle the problem of violence and antisocial behaviour on the streets at 2 a.m. when the clubs closed. As many pointed out, it was an absurd argument. I can remember fragments of conversations with friends and colleagues at the time and no-one in my recollection had expressed enthusiasm for the idea, although Monica did start coming home in high spirits in the middle of the night once in a while. The general consensus was that if those so inclined were given the opportunity to drink more freely, surely they would become more drunk and less concerned with respectful behaviour on the street.

The real motive behind the legislation emerged, that twenty-four hour drinking was a measure to try to buoy up an ailing economy. The hope was that it would present entrepreneurial opportunities to the licensing trade and offer service jobs for the marginalised sections of society. Primarily it would be a great revenue raiser for a government committed to not raising income tax. It was one's duty to drink for Britain.

Despite blanket advertising of all alcoholic drinks at every opportunity everywhere you could advertise alcoholic drinks, it didn't work out that way. Drink sales rose only slightly. Regardless of a proliferation of new bars and clubs, opened by wide boys and fly-by-nights hoping to cash in, many people stayed in as they had always done, not drinking, or perhaps buying the odd bottle of wine or pack of premium lager with their shopping at the supermarket. A majority of the population were responsible citizens at heart, still interested in family life or concerned with the practicalities of getting up in the morning and going to work. Clubbing remained the preserve of those under twenty-five with few commitments. I am over twenty five and Monica's occasional friskiness aside, twenty four hour licensing did not initially affect me that much.

But matters did not end there. Despite widespread protests from the medical profession, Muslims, pregnant women, diabetics and those living in areas where there were pubs and clubs The *New Licensing Act*, phased in over a six-month period last year, makes it compulsory to partake. Everyone under 65, regardless of gender, race, religion, occupation or financial circumstances is now required to go out *clubbing* at least once a week - or face a fixed penalty fine of £400. Prisoners and those in secure mental institutions are exempt. While exemptions are also in theory possible for others, for example, the blind or terminally ill, the application forms for an exemption certificate have apparently not yet become available.

Being under 65 and not blind or so far as I know terminally ill, the new licencing legislation began to affect me. Not least because Monica started coming home less frequently, and then not at all. But here is the real killer clause. If I have not consumed the necessary weekly units in one of the approved establishments by Thursday, I have to attend one of several new clubs on the High Street opened to cater for drink-dodgers, and drink my quota there, or pay the fine, deductible at source from my salary. The simultaneous introduction of identity cards simplified the administration. A central database now keeps track of each individual's consumption throughout the week. Thursday night is now the busiest night of the week everywhere as like me, many others struggle to meet their target.

The DirectGov leaflet, DD17 spells out my options. I can drink a dozen designer bottles (DNA, KGB, WKD, Colaholic, etc.), thirteen pints of Guinness, ten pints of Strongbow, eight cans of Special Brew, three bottles of wine, ten double vodkas or ten doubles of another spirit. All equally unpleasant in my opinion. I generally opt for ten double absinthes in a half litre glass. This way I can get the business over with and be back on the street throwing up outside the bus station by about 2. 30, and be on the earliest *clubbers bus*, which leaves at 2.45. It also represents the cheapest option. Ten designer bottles in *Scuffles* would set me back at least £60, whereas ten double absinthes in a half litre glass costs a mere £30. I did email the Home Office website, suggesting I just send a cheque each week for the £30, but the reply I received ignored the request and threatened me with court proceedings.

The cab waiting outside for me is a *DriveU2Drink* taxi. *DriveU2Drink* is a cab company employed to help facilitate compulsory clubbing. I throw on a tracksuit, breeze through a brisk bathroom routine, turn off the ambient CD of ocean sounds I use to help me sleep, put the anxious cat out, and make it to the cab, all in about sixty seconds.

It is my usual driver, Bryn. Bryn is not a man who finds it easy to relax.

'Ten minutes, I've been waiting out here boyo,' he says, lighting a cigarette from the one he is just finishing. 'It's not like I haven't got other calls to make.'

He looks me up and down disapprovingly.

'And I do not think they will let you into *Scuffles* dressed like that.'

'Everyone wears sports clothes in clubs,' I protest.

'Not tracksuits like that, they don't. It looks like it came from *Home-Bargains*. Where's the logo? You'll have to go and change, and remember that the meter is running.'

I don't anticipate that Bryn will be keen to stop on the way for me to get a kebab from *Tariqs'*, so I grab a slice of carrot cake from the fridge to provide something to help absorb the alcohol.

I live on the Rolf Harris estate in the suburbs, for the time being at least until my divorce from Monica comes through (or the estate gets renamed following recent allegations), and the town centre is a four mile drive. Bryn uses the distance to rant about the price of petrol, Eastern Europeans, asylum seekers, chavs, hoodies, smackheads, crackheads, gays, Blacks, Asians, speed limits, traffic calming, the royal family, the police, and modern art.

Having just taken up a post as a community worker, I wonder if I should take him up on some of his prejudices. As we drive on, I feel that there would be little point. His enmity seems to be free-floating. He could just as easily be ranting about the NHS, schools, social workers, Yanks, Chinese, transsexuals, celebrities in space or whatever is on the front page of his tabloid today.

We drive past Corporation Square, the hub of the sprawling *Tokers End* council estate. Around *Betterbet* there is a lively throng of locals keen on getting a bet on the night football, or as *Betterbet* is next to *Bruisers' Bar*, perhaps the Mauler-Stitch bare-knuckle fight from the *Milton Keynes Colosseum*. Betting Tax has recently been reintroduced, but is proving not to deter punters. And as compulsory lotto and compulsory scratch cards have been such a success, compulsory betting is now being considered as another means to boost government coffers. The residents of *Tokers End* are clearly ahead of the game. They need little encouragement.

'They will bet on anything, see,' says Bryn. 'The Christmas number one, the Christmas number two, the discovery of life on Mars, the pope to break a leg skiing, The Finnish Wife Carrying Championship, where the next terrorist attack will be, how many will be killed in the next hurricane.'

'I know someone that bets on virtual horse racing,' I say.

'Look you,' says Bryn. 'My next door neighbour *trains* virtual horses. He tells me that when you buy a virtual horse, the fitness level is only about fifty percent. This increases by between two to five percent each time you train it, see. He trains his virtual horses six times a day.'

I nod, trying not to get crumbs of carrot cake on the floor. Perhaps the recipe would benefit from an extra egg.

'How are things between you and the missus?' asks Bryn, breaking off from his tirade.

I confide that things are not good. That Monica is *staying with friends*, and that letters between *Hoffman, Cohen and Partners* and *Gallagher, Dreamer and Shed* are arriving daily.

'Tough business, I can sympathise with you boyo.' says Bryn. 'I had the same thing with Tegwyn, see. Tegwyn liked the pop too. I had to sell the Beamer, you know. Heavy shit, the drink. You cannot imagine how much I hate this fucking job.'

*Stacey is a single mum. Her daughter, Jade is three years old. Stacey is forced to take the DriveU2Drink cab one Thursday night to fulfil her obligation. She has no babysitter. She cannot afford one. All her dispos- able income goes on her weekly night out. While Stacey is at Moonies, Jade burns herself on the electric hob. The neighbours hear Jade's screams, break the door down and phone for an ambulance. They phone Stacey on the number that they have been given, but Stacey cannot hear the phone over the thumping jungle music. In years gone by, Social Services would have become involved in a case like this. There is no talk of prosecution. Stacey's case is summarily brushed under the carpet. There are many Staceys. There is probably one living next door to you, so, if you do not have to go out drinking on Thursday nights, be vigilant.*

We drive on, the details of Bryn's divorce passing in one ear and out the other. The overturned Passat outside *The Cold Store* suggests that little has improved in *Tokers End* over the past week, but at least the council have removed the burnt out police car from outside the housing office. The ten foot high supermarket trolley and paint can sculpture adds a spark of interest to the drab paved area, taking attention away from the mountain of polystyrene fast food containers in the overgrown planters. Bryn takes a right into *Bob Marley Avenue* to avoid the traffic calming on *Malcolm X Street*. The boarded up windows of the Lebanese café on the corner boasts a selection of new spray can art, some of it quite colourful and creative. Art of the state, I believe it is now called. The overall effect is unfortunately compromised by the puerile fascination of less talented taggers for obscenity. Budgens' supermarket, which has over the years suffered more than most from graffiti and vandalism, now has a large red sign saying *closed until further notice* and the premises of *Accessible Finance* next door thanks to a recent ram raid has become accessible to all. A row of clamped cars outside the *Baghdad House* flats suggests the police were round earlier as part of their crackdown on expired tax discs. Even the Tokers End Community Centre minibus is clamped.

I remember, almost fondly now, the time that Monica and I were clamped several years ago when we were shopping in Soho. We still had the Cosworth then, so it must have been before the gallery went bust. Just after the *Diane Arbus* exhibition. It was after the loss of the gallery that Monica started drinking. ..... I wonder what she is doing now. We haven't spoken since the solicitors became involved. She will not be happy with Giancarlo. She will always play second fiddle to his Maserati, or his Alfa Romeo, or whatever car he is playing around with in his workshop, and he is nearly twice her age.

'Hard not to be bitter, you know what I mean,' says Bryn.

I hadn't realised we were still having the same conversation. I agree, bitter is part of what I feel, but I do miss her.

We stop at the temporary traffic lights on Karl Jenkins Way where they are building the new twenty four hour retail park to replace the recently demolished factories. A lengthy wait in a long line of other *DriveU2Drink* and *BoozeCruise* cabs gives Bryn the opportunity to acquaint me with just how many famous Welsh people there have been: David Lloyd George, Dylan Thomas, Richard Burton, Anthony Hopkins, Tom Jones, Shirley Bassey and Charlotte Church to name but a few. The relative obscurity of his other nominees does not seem to help his case, leaving me with the thought that perhaps the Welsh are not cut out for fame.

The lights eventually change and we move on past the HSBC Hospital and the John Lewis Primary School towards the centre of town. Bryn points out the *Lost Cause* public house, hidden away behind a battalion of mobile phone masts.

'The only pub in town that still allows smoking,' he says, lighting up another cigarette. 'They've turned the inside into the outside.'

Smoking is banned in the workplace of course and this includes restaurants and bars and, it occurs to me, taxis too. The government's attitude to smoking is, some cynics feel, a missed opportunity. Compulsory smoking in public places would bring in heaps of revenue for the Chancellor, and help to pay the escalating bill of our foreign conflicts. By bringing in more revenue and systematically reducing the number of claimants, promotion of tobacco might also have also help to tackle the pensions crisis. Legislation of a few class B or C substances as well, with a little favourable promotion, might finance an invasion of some more middle eastern countries to help secure our supplies of oil and gas.

I don't watch the news very much, in fact, I hardly watch television at all. Monica succumbed to the Sky advertising early on and I still have a choice of about four hundred channels, but if I have some spare time in the evening I prefer to work on one of my stories on the computer.

'Why do you always write about ghosts?' Monica used to say. 'All of that went out with Harry Potter. And nobody wants to know about your dreams. There's no money to be made in that supernatural stuff.'

'There's no money to be made in watching *Celebrity Love Triangle* night after night,' I may have replied. 'It's not about the money.' But of course, it was about the money. After the gallery closed, Monica showed no signs of wanting to go out and earn any.

'Tegwyn used to have these visions, see,' says Bryn returning the focus to his own marital breakdown. 'I suppose you could say she lost touch with reality. I thought it was the drink, like. But then they put her on this new medication and she could see into the future. She would say something like, Idris is going to win eighteen million on the lottery - and it would happen. Exactly eighteen million, Idris won. One day not long before she left she said, 'I can see increasing signs of unrest. When's that going to happen, Tegwen? I remember saying.' 'twenty fifteen,' she said. And here we are.'

*Wayne was allergic to alcohol. Drinking brought him out in hives and affected his breathing. Although Wayne was diagnosed with anaphylaxis early on, he found over the years that he could manage the odd glass of wine at a function without major effects. However, when faced with the compulsory Thursday night binge at WhiteRiot his breathing became constricted and he collapsed by the bar. Collapsing by the bar was not so unusual here, so there was a delay before he was attended to by the stewards and taken to hospital. Held up further by the Thursday night mayhem in the streets and with the Thursday night bottleneck at A and E, he died waiting to see a consultant. You will know someone with alcohol intolerance. Keep an eye on them when they have to meet their weekly target.*

As we approach the outskirts of town the streets shows increasing signs of unrest. Bryn's radio operator spits staccato messages to let the drivers know which streets to avoid. Even so, each bar we pass had a noisy mob of hammered hooded hooligans outside taking advantage of all night happy hours. The smoking ban inside licensed premises has served to promote large unruly alfresco gatherings. We can hear loud urban music coming from every direction. Gangs of pale six-foot pro-wrestlers, with shaved heads, tattooed biceps, and rings hanging from their ears, eyes and noses parade chanting and singing. Black youths are taunting Asian youths and Asians are taunting blacks in front of a bank of CCTV cameras. The gold jewellery on display looks like it could be an advert for El Dorado. An air of uncontrolled mayhem reigns. Fights are breaking out here and there between groups decked out in rival brands of leisure wear. It is like a noisy playground where the children have just become older. The muted wailing of police and ambulance sirens is continuous and we have to pull over several times on *Eminem Street* to let emergency vehicles pass. Outside *Blazes*, a predatory gang of teenage girls with short skirts and large bare waists swigging out of pink bottles shaped like penises shout and swear at a gang of teenage girls with shorter skirts and larger bare waists, swigging out of red bottles shaped like penises. Bryn tries to negotiate a path through the two groups of marauding youngsters. Missiles fly through the air as the two gangs meet. We are caught in the crossfire and a pink penis narrowly misses the windscreen of the cab. The red penis, which follows it, is more accurate and a large crack appears in Bryn's line of vision. Instinctively he winds his window down and hurls some abuse. Ill-advisedly, I feel. Next thing we know, a writhing mass of tattooed teenage flesh is all over the cab. The girls scream madly, baseball bats smashing against glass. The cab follows an uncertain path down *Cameron Street* towards the *Thatcher Monument* as it was rocked up and down. Several vehicles coming toward us collided, there was some kind of explosion, and that is as much as I can remember.

The HSBC Hospital is nowhere near the top of the Daily Telegraph Performance League Table, but there again it is not near the bottom. It is at 106 out of 187 hospitals in the *Mortality Rating*. It could be argued that the figures are a little skewed by the fact that the HSBC has borne the brunt of last year's fish flu epidemic. It is still well ahead of The KFC Hospital and The Vodafone Hospital in its average waiting time at A&E, just four and a half hours. After midnight on Thursday this, of course, rises fourfold. The Telegraph's ratings show that the HSBC's record of successful operations is below the national average, and it is 123 out of 187 for cases MRSA, but perhaps all of this is beside the point. The hospital's reputation is built primarily on being a leader in experimental research.

Anyway, whatever its merits, it is in the HSBC Hospital that I find myself. I don't remember if I have signed any forms of consent but I have been placed on a programme to test an experimental new drug called *Contradil*.

While the manufacturers are hailing *Contradil* as something of a universal panacea, tests have revealed that it might not be without side effects. Among the documented side effects are sweating, dizziness, visual disturbances, sickness, nausea and mood swings. Among the undocumented side effects are paranoia, time disorientation, loss of reason, inability to stay awake, and vivid dreams.

Dr Black is injecting me with plasticine. The room has the warped geometry of a Maurits Escher painting. It is one of many in a large gothic house that is both familiar and unfamiliar. It is at once my school, my parental home, and my workplace. But still I do not know my way around and it is dark. I am anxious because I am late for something. I have missed an exam or an appointment and am searching for clarity. The corridor is charged with the bitter aroma of absinthe. On a large screen, gangs of pale six-foot pro-wrestlers, with shaved heads, tattooed biceps, and rings hanging from their ears, eyes and noses parade chanting and singing. There is a commentary. I recognise the voice. It is my own, but my speech is slurred. I climb up a flight of stairs that takes me downward. I become immersed suddenly in a pool of clear warm saliva. Hank Williams is singing a song about being chained and manacled. I begin humming along to the tune. Someone joins in on the harmonica. They wanted to harm Monica. I am in a different room now; this one is long and narrow like a gallery. Its walls are of weathered blocked stone as if they should be outer walls. I struggle on my hands and knees along a row of Diane Arbus photographs, which keep changing. I know the people in some of the photographs, but their faces are stretched into grotesque caricatures. Now I am in another room, an upstairs room with an exaggeratedly concave ceiling. I go through a small gnarled wooden door and find myself in a grey corridor. It is damp and water trickles down the walls. I switch on a torch and there are bugs the size of rats on the floor, and rats the size of cats. Petrified, I make it to the other end of the corridor, where I crawl through the eye of a Lebanese hunchback. I find myself in white open space with a transparent green and magenta yin yang motif window hanging from a tree. I peel a large succulent peach. Now I am on a golden beach listening to the gentle echo of summer voices. A woman with long dark hair and iridescent tantric tattoos who I met on a balloon trip is rubbing oil into my back and talking in soft Italian. A man in a harlequin suit with a limp is selling doughnuts, and dwarf camels, as small as cats, are frolicking around pyramids that children have made in the sand. A car outside my window sounds its horn three times.

# GUN

Bors Ryman works as a tyre technician in the old mining town of Camborne in Cornwall. Most evenings after work, he picks up his girlfriend, Suzi Foxx from outside *HairCraft* salon and takes her to *The Cock Inn*. They have a bite to eat, play pool, darts or dominoes and chat with the regulars about rugby. Most girls that Bors has known have found the pubs he likes to frequent a little unsophisticated. They have shown little interest in rugby, or darts, or dominoes for that matter. Because of this, his previous romances have never lasted long, but he has been seeing Suzi for several weeks.

Bors himself does not play much rugby these days. After all, he will be forty soon and rugby is a game for younger and fitter men. But he likes to go and watch his team, Camborne RFC, especially when they are having a good run. They are currently having a bad run, due to the loss of their fly half, John Scorer and their blindside flanker, Trev Padstow. No one is sure what happened to the pair. They mysteriously disappeared halfway through the season. Camborne have only won one game since.

Having been thrown out of his accommodation over rent arrears, Bors is staying at his friend, Breok's, this despite Breok supporting Camborne's great rivals Redruth RFC. Suzi's flatmate Tamsyn apparently does not like the idea of Bors staying over. The flat is too small for that kind of thing, she says. So, after their chilli con carne or chicken and chips and a pint or two of cloudy Cornish cyder at *The Cock*, once or twice a week Bors and Suzi get their rocks off in his Mitsubishi Lancer. He has made it more comfortable with a duck feather duvet and pillows, a can of California car scent and a DVD player with cinema surround sound.

It is on one such occasion in the car park behind Tesco that a gun falls out of Suzi's handbag. At first, Bors thinks it is her phone that has dropped down between the seats. Suzi often loses her phone. It is not until after they have finished their business in the back seat that he realises that it is a gun. Guns are quite unusual in Cornwall. Bors has never seen one before. This is the type he understands from the movies to be a semi-automatic pistol.

'Fucking hell, Suzi!' he says. 'What's going on?'

'Oh. Don't worry about that,' says Suzi. 'It's ...... only a toy. It's a present for ..... my colleague, Hannah's son, er, Vincent. He will be ten next week.'

Bors picks it up. It does not feel to him like a toy gun. It seems too heavy and has too much detail. He remarks on this.

'They are very realistic these days, aren't they?' says Suzi, taking it from him and slipping it back in her bag. 'But, I suppose that is the point.'

'But.....,' he begins.

Suzi does not let him finish. She is practised at the art of distraction. When it comes down to it she finds Bors is the same as all other men she has been with. They might just as well have an on off button.

While Suzi has not been in the habit of lying to him, the incident begins to sew the seeds of doubt in Bors's mind. On the way home, after dropping Suzi off, he is unable to rid himself of the thought that it might have been a real pistol and that Suzi may be concealing something sinister from him. What does he really know about her? He knows she is twenty nine – or thereabouts. She has a fleur-de-lys tattoo on her thigh and she is a Gemini. She takes more of an interest in sport than most women do and even seems to understand the rules of rugby.

He knows nothing about her background. He has a vague recollection of her saying early on in their relationship that both her parents were dead, although he cannot be sure. You don't take in everything that someone says early on in a relationship because you are more concerned with getting your own biography across. He knows from her accent that she is not from Cornwall but he is not good at placing dialects and she has never offered any details of her origins. She appears to have no children and has never mentioned any brothers or sisters. Sometimes, without being specific, she has alluded to former lovers, and so far as he can tell is not without experience in amatory matters. But for a woman of ...... let's say thirty three, on the surface Suzi Foxx comes without obvious baggage.

When Bors goes to pick up Suzi outside *HairCraft*, the following day she is not there. Normally she is outside waiting for him. He waits impatiently on the double yellows just down the road but still she does not arrive. He decides to park the Lancer and go in to remind Suzi that he is here. Maybe one of her hair appointments arrived late or something. He might get the opportunity to check out Hannah at the same time and perhaps ask her about Vincent and his birthday. A gun does seem to be a strange kind of present in these days of drug gangs and terrorism.

'I'm sorry but we don't have anyone called Suzi working here,' says the alarmingly young receptionist. 'I'm Teegan. Can I help?'

Bors realises he has never actually been into the salon before. Suzi always had him wait outside. 'Is Hannah here then?' he asks, out of desperation.

'We have no-one called Hannah here either,' Teegan says. 'You could try the *Pound Stretcher* shop next door.'

Bors tries her phone. It is switched off. It is nearly half past six. He makes his way to *The Cock Inn*. He is not sure what the misunderstanding is, but surely Suzi will turn up there, full of apologies.

'No Suzi, tonight then, Bors?' says Big Hank. Hank is the one who arranges the monthly country and western nights at *The Cock*. Once a month he dresses like Roy Rogers and rides to the pub on his horse and tethers it up outside. *You can't be done for drinking and driving with a horse*, he says each time. The joke is now a little stale.

'I expect Suzi will be in later,' says Bors.

'Like that, is it?' says Jago. Jago is the dominoes champion at *The Cock*. He is quite possibly the only one who understands the scoring, or perhaps he makes up the rules as he goes along. All that Bors knows is that he has never beaten him.

'She's trouble, that one,' says Hank.

'Better off without her if you ask me,' says Jago.

'No one's asking you,' says Bors.

'The guys are right, Bors. I don't think that you can trust her,' says Bodmin Bob the barman. 'I saw her at Newquay Airport today. She was catching a flight. Düsseldorf, I think it was.' Bodmin Bob has just returned from London, having done some business there. While everyone agrees that Bodmin Bob is dodgy, no one is quite sure what his business is. Some think that he is a drug dealer while others think he is a fraudster. There is even speculation that he is a people trafficker or a hit man. No-one can explain why he is working as a barman at

*The Cock.*

Bors can't remember Suzi mentioning any plans to go to Germany. While he has to admit he sometimes switches off when she is talking, especially if he is watching a game, he is almost sure he would have remembered something like that. While he still wants to think the best of Suzi, what with the gun and the hairdressers and now this, it is becoming increasingly difficult. He doesn't want to lose face here in the bar, though. Not in front of Big Hank and Jago. He will never live it down.

'Ah, I've just remembered,' he says, in a flash of inspiration. 'Suzi's sister Heidi lives in Dusseldorf. And it's her son Vincent's birthday tomorrow. He will be ten. I remember her buying the present for him.'

'That's nice,' says Hank. 'What did she buy him?'

He is about to say a gun, but catches himself. 'A rugby shirt,' he says instead. 'A Phil Scrummer number 8 jersey.

'They play a lot of rugby in Dusseldorf, do they?' says Jago.

'She should have bought him a gun,' says Hank. 'Ten year old boys like guns.'

After leaving *The Cock*, Bors drives round to the address that Suzi has given him for her and Tamsyn's flat. He knocks loudly. He is determined to find out what is going on and if he can't get the information from Suzi, then he will be able to get it from Tamsyn. The burly wrestler type that answers the door is visibly unhappy at being disturbed by a drunken dolt, claims no knowledge of the pair and instructs Bors to leave forthwith before he punches his lights out. His girlfriend's web of lies appears to be extending.

Over the next few days, Bors keeps a low profile. There is no word from Suzi Foxx and her phone stays switched off. He is disappointed, embarrassed and angry. He does not like being made a fool of. He keeps his distance from Breok, and at work, he indignantly greets customers and changes their tyres with extreme prejudice. He steers clear of *The Cock Inn*. He doesn't even go along to Big Hank's Country and Western night. He gives Camborne RFC's final home game of the season against Redruth, said to be the fiercest rivalry in rugby, a miss. He isn't even aware of the mysterious disappearance of Camborne winger, Will Wilson, before the game. Missing Will's dynamic runs, Camborne lose by a single point and as a result face relegation.

Breok has always found that people in this neck of the woods usually have the courtesy to knock when they come round to visit. Equally SWAT team raids are unusual in Cornwall are so he is doubly shocked when early one morning such a team forces its way into his house using a battering ram.

'Hands in the air!' screams the officer with the Breaking Bad beard.

'Where is she?' hollers the one wearing Men In Black sunglasses.

'Who?' asks Breok. This meets with a blow to the head from the one with the Die Hard facial scars.

'What's the fuck's going on?' asks Bors, emerging groggily from his room. This meets with a blow to the head from Samuel L. Jackson.

'We're looking for Clara Hess. That's who,' yells Jean Claude Van Damme. 'Now! Where is she?'

'Who? What?' says Breok. He appears to be adjusting to his new role of crime suspect quickly.

'We know that she has been at this address, knucklehead,' shouts Breaking Bad beard. 'Keep your hands in the air.'

The other four begin to roam, methodically trashing the place, tipping over furniture, tossing Breok's belongings here and there, as if Clara Hess might be hiding behind the bookcase, in the closet, under the settee, in the fridge.

'Why are you wrecking my flat?' says Breok. 'We have never heard of the person you are looking for. Where did you get this information?'

'Aha! We have your friend Robert Trescothick in custody, birdbrain, and he has been very helpful,' sneers Breaking Bad beard.

'Who?' says Bors.

'Robert Trescothick, asshole.' says BBB. 'You might know him better as Bodmin Bob,'

Bors does not see Bob as one to co-operate with the police, but then you never know, do you? There's not a great amount of subtlety with this bunch. And, of course, they may have caught Bob red handed doing whatever it is that he does. But who is this Clara Hess, and where does she fit in? He reflects that it is safer if for the moment he pretends he does not know Bodmin Bob. This is a miscalculation. It earns him a hefty blow to the midriff from Die Hard, who has just returned to the fray.

'Look here, smartass,' he says. 'You have two choices. Come down to the station and tell us what you know or come down to the station and we turn off the cameras and the tape and give you a good kicking.'

At this point Bors wants to mention solicitors, but a fist in the windpipe prevents him. There is a sudden crackle on Breaking Bad beard's radio, an unintelligible voice barks something through the static. Die Hard turns around. BBB hollers something in a cryptic language that probably only armed officers are able to understand. It seems to hail a change of plan. Without further explanation the SWAT team vanishes.

'Did all of that really happen?' asks Breok.

'It certainly feels like it did,' says Bors.

'Must have got the wrong house, don't you think?' says Breok.

Bors is not so sure. He does not mention it to Breok but he has the growing feeling that Suzi Foxx and Clara Hess might be one and the same. He is not even sure any more about Breok. When something like this happens you do not know what to think. To take himself off the radar he decides to go to stay at a local bed and breakfast until it all blows over.

When later on he sees the headline in *The Cornishman* 'CAMBORNE RUGBY STAR FOUND DEAD ON BODMIN MOOR' he begins to suspect that the SWAT team's inept raid might have been in connection with this. The report says the body of Will Wilson is believed to have been lying in the undergrowth for several days before being discovered by a local man out walking his dog. ...... Wilson is believed to have been shot several times by an automatic pistol ..... Police are combing the area ...... They are also investigating whether there might be a connection with the disappearance of Camborne's other two rugby stars earlier in the season. .... No trace of them was ever found .... Anyone who might have any information that might be of help in tracing the killer is being asked to contact .........

The next few days bring some startling disclosures. Two more bodies are found on Bodmin Moor, fitting the description of John Scorer and Trev Padstow, the two missing Camborne rugby stars. Bodmin Bob is released without charge. Breok along with Clara Hess and several others whose names are not familiar face are arrested and face charges of murder or conspiracy to commit murder. It is all over the papers. At work they are all talking about it. There is much speculation about the possible motive. Rumours are rife. A rival rugby team, Redruth or Launceston perhaps? The Devon Mafia? A European takeover? Everyone seems to have heard a whisper somewhere.

Bors does not know how to respond. In a way, he feels very close to it all. He might have seen this coming with Suzi Foxx or Clara Hess or whoever she was, but never in a million years would he have suspected that his friend, Breok would be involved. Breok Trevanian, the skinny lad from Tolcarne a gunman, unthinkable? He has known Breok since his school days. He cannot bring himself to look at the *Cornishman* report and especially not the pictures of them being taken into custody.

'Hands up mister,' says a small voice behind him, as he is leaving work.

Bors turns around to see a young lad pointing a gun at him, a semi-automatic pistol. The boy is laughing. Out of the corner of his eye, he catches a glimpse of Suzi Foxx wearing a summer print dress walking towards him.

'Hello Bors,' she says sheepishly. 'Put that thing away, Vincent! .... It's all right, Bors. It's not a real gun, but they look so realistic these days, don't they? ........ Hey! I'm sorry about all the trouble that I've caused you. I know I shouldn't have lied about everything. The thing is I couldn't tell you much before because ......... Well, if you'd like to come round to my new flat later, I'll tell you then. ....... Oh, this is my son Vincent by the way.'

# The Devil's Interval

I have not always been a killer. I blame my descent into malevolence and murder on Holst and Wagner. Oh! And Black Sabbath. Mostly Black Sabbath, in fact. Perhaps I had better explain. It all began when in February 1970, I was listening to a Dutch radio station late at night with my friend Ray. We were both eighteen. We had just moved into our first flat. We had come back from *The Cellar Bar* and had just finished a big fat spliff. It was a stormy night with the wind rattling the shutters.

On the stroke of midnight out of the static of the night-time radio, soared an apocalyptic new track. It was like nothing I had heard before. It was hypnotic, sinister, demonic. Four stinging chords on the guitar repeated over and over with a screaming vocal. But what chords they were! This was music from the very depths of Hell. We caught on straight away that something was happening, but to paraphrase Bob Dylan, we did not know what it was.

'Far out,' said Ray. 'It's badass. ......... But at the same time, I'm a little scared.'

'I know what you mean,' I said. 'It's like a thunder cloud blotting out the sun. It's really cool, but you know that something real bad is going to happen.'

What was happening was, in fact, the birth of heavy metal music. It all started here at this very moment. At the tail end of the sixties, music had been heading in this direction with The Jeff Beck Group and Led Zeppelin, but their music was tame, legitimate by comparison. This was the real deal. The Dutch station we were listening to played the music with no DJ's babble, but I managed to find out the following day that this was the title track from Black Sabbath's eponymous album.

Much later I was to discover that the secret behind the track lay is something known as the diabolus in musica or The Devil's Interval. The diabolus in musica was considered so ominous in the Middle Ages that it was banned by clerics for fear it would raise Lucifer himself. It consists of a tritone (augmented fourth or diminished fifth) and spanning as it does three tones, the interval violates a musical convention and sounds dissonant, producing an unsettling feeling in the listener. Playing the note of C followed by F sharp somehow encapsulates the essence of evil. Black Sabbath may have stumbled on this accidentally, but they were not the first in the modern era to use it. Wagner used it in *Götterdämmerung* and Holst used it in *Mars - The Bringer of War*.

The difference perhaps is that these two classical greats were fully aware of what they were doing. Dissonance was precisely the effect they were after. There were, of course, no stoned freaks listening to late night Dutch radio stations in their day whose lives might be driven off course by The Devil's Interval. Wagner and Holst had only the hoi polloi as an audience and many of these were beyond redemption anyway, involved as they were in either military manoeuvres and empire building.

I bought the album, *Black Sabbath* and over the next few weeks Ray and I played it over and over at deafening volume. Ray had just bought a powerful NAD amplifier and some Wharfedale speakers and this punched the satanic sound around the small front room of the basement flat, through the whole house, up the street and possibly the next town. Dozens of stoned freaks dropped by to listen and went off to buy the album. In no time at all *Black Sabbath* was the one of the three albums they carried around with them and rolled their joints on.

I can't say for certain whether the tritone repeated over and over was a factor in the landlord's suicide. We were so taken over by the music that we did not realise that he had gone. We just thought it odd that he hadn't been round to collect the rent. I cannot claim therefore that this was the beginning of my killing spree. This did not really take off until years later.

If you've ever been to a Black Sabbath concert you will know what I'm talking about when I say that it can instigate feelings of violence. I felt rancour and malevolence to the very core of my being when I saw them play live at Malvern Winter Gardens. It was lucky I didn't get arrested for flattening the bouncer. The Devil's Interval resounded in my head for hours after the show. I was wired. I could not get rid of the feeling. On the way home I punched the taxi driver. After this, Ray insisted that we give Black Sabbath a break for a while.

I met Linda and she carefully monitored of my heavy metal music listening, and for years, I managed to keep a lid on my violent tendencies. Linda was a nurse and knew people who might be able to help me.

'You're doing very well, Martin,' my anger management counsellor, Hortense would say. 'It's been months since you hit anyone.'

I got married and did the things you do when that happens, bought a house, went to dinner parties, had children, slept with my wife's best friend and got divorced. Ray met Mary and did the same, in fact, most of my friends did the same. It was never going to work, was it? It was a generational thing. I'm sure Linda and Mary slept with our best friends too but didn't tell us. This was what happened back then.

'At least you've got that out of your system, Martin,' Hortense would say. 'Now you need to get on with your life.'

It was now the late seventies. Freed from responsibility, I felt the need for some more heavy metal music. Although punk had taken over mainstream rock music, fortunately, there was also a burgeoning choice of very loud heavy metal bands to listen to. If anything the volume had been turned up. These bands needed LGVs to carry their kit around. Many of them had also discovered the potency of The Devil's Interval. I went to see Judas Priest play at Cheltenham Town Hall. They used the devastating tritone over and over in their set. I began to feel the violent impulses again. After the concert, I went on the rampage. I set about a complete stranger and impaled him on the trident in Neptune's Fountain. While I was only charged with manslaughter, custody threatened to put a halt to my appreciation of heavy metal.

Thanks to a glowing report from Hortense I got off with a ten year stretch and was out again in five. There were now so many metal bands that I didn't know where to start, ACDC, Metallica, Iron Maiden, Motorhead, Slayer, Megadeth, Def Leppard to name but a few. And amazingly Black Sabbath were still going. Hortense recommended that if I did listen to them I should do so with the volume down and under no circumstances should I go to a gig. She lent me some Al Stewart cassettes to listen to. I was not impressed. He sounded too posh to make meaningful music. Next, she tried me on Billy Joel. He was even worse, a real pussy. I was pleased when my machine chewed up the tape.

It is never easy for ex-prisoners to find work, so I was overjoyed when after a few weeks of twiddling my thumbs and feeling depressed I managed to get a job in a musical instrument repair workshop. The manager of *Black Keys*, Matt Black gave me a chance. I think he sympathised with my plight because his son, Jett had himself been in trouble.

Matt Black explained the rudiments of music to me. He taught me about scales, chromatics and dissonance. It was Matt who told me about the Devil's Interval. It was just my bad luck that he continued to demonstrate it. *The Planets* apparently was his favourite piece of music and *Mars* was his favourite section of it. He played it on repeat in the workshop. At least this is how it appeared. Perhaps I had developed earworm, but as I rubbed the glue into the crack on the cello neck, the dissonance of Holst's diabolus in musica echoed endlessly in my head. The frightening crescendo kept building until I could take no more. I brought the instrument down on Matt's skull.

My barrister, Conway Clifford Junior buckled when he found out who was presiding over the case. Judge Bearcroft was notorious for his no-nonsense stance. The old curmudgeon was variously rumoured to have jailed people for loitering, for not wearing a seat belt and for stealing pencils from the office. He described me as a ferocious animal that needed to be caged. Hortense's mitigation regarding the diabolus in musica fell flat. Judge Bearcroft had a low tolerance for musical mumbo jumbo and he gave me a twenty.

I was out in ten, just in time for the Black Sabbath Reunion Tour. The publicity promised that they were going to play louder than ever. They did. Much louder. And *Black Sabbath* the key number in their set was deafening. The tritone echoed around the auditorium like a battle raging. I know I shouldn't have gone. And I know I shouldn't have killed Hortense. And it would be foolish to deny the connection. My rage was clearly a result of those demonic chords rattling round in my head. It was the Devil's work all right. With no-one to mitigate my plea, this time, I got life.

I am a few years into my sentence. I was in Wandsworth at first, which was tough, but as prisoner numbers rose I got moved to Belmarsh, which is not quite so bad. I share my cell with Denzel, another lifer. Denzel was a big name in gangland in the early eighties. One of the characters in the film, *The Long Good Friday* was based on him. Denzel has been in here a while. It shows in his demeanour. He is massively overweight. We chat about Staffordshire bull terriers and Millwall FC.

I have got what others might consider a cushy job working in the prison library. The problem I have is that the library is right next to the Prison Governor's office and Governor Kraut keeps playing Wagner, more specifically *Götterdämmerung*. Why is he doing it? Doesn't he know about The Devil's Interval? Isn't he aware of my history, or is the bastard just trying to wind me up? I nearly killed Nolan Rocco yesterday in the canteen. I had my hands around his throat. What stopped me? It certainly wasn't Floyd Edmondson. Big Floyd was egging me on. What stopped me was the thought that maybe one day I might be able to get out of here, but I know I won't. Judge Block told me that life would mean life. And with the diabolus in musica pulsing round in my head, it is surely only a matter of time before I kill someone else.

# A Stone's Throw From The Beach

Lastminuteholidays.com did not actually specify that Sea View had a view of the sea, but there again it did not say that it didn't. The default position, you would have thought, was that it did, especially as there were pictures of the waves rolling in on a clear sandy beach in the post. I ought to have checked on Google Maps. I would have seen then that Sea View was, in fact, several miles inland and unlikely to be *a stone's throw from the beach* as advertised on the site. I did not check because I was too busy at work and Diane and I were in a hurry to get away. We were going through a sticky patch in our marriage. Looking at the reviews on *Trip Advisor* in the prison library now only adds to the feeling of regret. The highest rating Sea View was given was 1 star.

A glance at customer feedback would have let me know that the view consisted of a popular fly tipping site, a dumping ground for broken furniture, white goods and sundry household waste. Scrap vehicles and even an old crane had been abandoned and left to rust. A bonfire of car tyres smouldered day and night. Security was also flagged up as an issue. The front door to the apartment did not even close. According to the comments, it had been that way for months. The twin beds were three-quarter length and there was no bedding. Several correspondents mentioned the stench of cabbage which was being boiled on an industrial scale in the kitchen below.

Our stay, which was to have been a week, confirmed all these points. It wouldn't have been so bad if the diesel generator had been a little further from our bedroom window. But, what really did it for me though was the noise from the building site nearby. To maximise the use of the supply of cheap immigrant labour in the area, the developer kept the pile driver going through the night.

When Diane and I first arrived at Sea View on that Saturday in July, horrified though we were, we decided we were going to make the best of it. After all, we were on holiday. And of course, we had some issues to work through. There was no sense in adding to these by getting into a state about the shortcomings of the accommodation. In any case, we could find no-one to complain to. We had paid the full week's rental up front and the owner saw no need to meet and greet us. And we needed no key as the door had no lock.

'We're not going to spend that much time indoors,' I said to Diane.

She agreed. 'I expect there's lots of interesting scenery around here,' she said. 'And we can probably drive out to the coast one day. I'm sure we could do it in under an hour.'

We probably *wouldn't* have spent any time indoors, had it not been for the persistent heavy rain that started just after we arrived. Every time we looked out of the window it was still raining. It was just a question of whether at any particular time it was easing off or getting harder. On the positive side, the rain did douse the smouldering heap of tyres. We could not watch TV as the set had already been stolen; there was just an aerial lead trailing from the socket which led to nowhere. I did not even bother getting my tablet out of the case as it was clear there was going to be no wi-fi.

I-Spy got us nowhere as there were not many things in the apartment to spy. The ones that there were could be guessed easily. W was window or wall and B was bed. F was for floor and C was for ceiling. There were no C to sit on and no T to sit at. There was no C or even an M to cook with and no F to put the food in.

After a sleepless Saturday night on the uncomfortable beds with the pile driver thumping away and the rain beating against the window, we spent the whole of Sunday at *The Goat and Bicycle*. The effects of the beer and the wine helped us to block out the disturbance from the building site on Sunday night. This was just as well, as in addition to the existing operations, I noticed they had now hired a centrifugal pump to get rid of the flood-water that had accumulated on the site.

It was still raining the following day so we drove, via several detours due to the river bursting its banks, to Littleton, a little town ten miles away. After lunch at *The Blind Monkey*, we saw all three films that were on offer at the *Roxy*. I wonder why it is that small town cinemas choose to screen the most violent films. *Saw* was followed by *Teeth* and these were reprised by *Maniac*. After this, our nerves in tatters, we went for a nightcap at *The Goat*.

This was the night it happened. The pile driver was beating out its dull rhythm. The generator was belching out its acrid fumes to supplement the pungent smell of stale cabbage from below. The rain turned to hail and Diane and I had the mother of all rows. She asked me why I was always so miserable. I said I wasn't. She said I was. I said that it wasn't her, I was unhappy at work, what with the shifts and all. She said that's no reason to take it out on her. I said I didn't. She said I did, and if my job caused me that much stress I should give it up. I said if I did we wouldn't be able to afford the payments on her new car, or little things like holidays. She said you mean holidays like this. I suggested she might think of getting a job. She said she had a job, clearing up after me and my bloody pigeons. If you want to keep pigeons why don't you go back oop north. She kept on pushing my buttons. I was weak. I was spineless. I had never satisfied her. ....... The pile driver kept on thumping. I felt murderous. I stormed off. I couldn't control myself. I had to take it out on somebody. I made straight for the building site and ....

Because of my standing in the community, I did not come under suspicion. At first, Diane told me I should give myself up, but after I agreed to get rid of the pigeons, she came round. I hadn't realised how much she hated my pigeons. Perhaps pigeons are not a woman's thing. But, now as I sit here browsing the internet in the prison library, I question whether I deserve to be at liberty. Am I any better that the people I have in my custody? Some of them are here for minor offences. Non-payment of council tax. Possession of cannabis. Shoplifting. And I think about what I've done. Sometimes my conscience wants me to come clean and admit that it was me who killed Iosif Petrescu that night back in July.

# Where's Your Car, Debbie?

'Where's your car, Debbie ...... Debbie where's your car,' screams a cracked voice. There is an air of desperation about it. It is coming from some distance away. It sounds like it is coming over a PA system in the park. As we approach, Betty and I notice that a large crowd has gathered to listen. There are now hundreds of people in the park, perhaps thousands. Earlier when we had a cup of tea at the café by the bowling green, the park was empty. Betty was saying how peaceful it was and wondered if we ought to bring a picnic down in the new basket that Bob and Ros bought her as a retirement present.

To find out what is happening, we ease our way forward through a throng of unkempt rebel youths. Many of them look no more than ten or twelve. But then most people look young to us these days. As we near the front, we see two tattooed men in vests jumping around on a makeshift stage. One of them is strangling an electric guitar while his friend is banging on a drum and shouting hysterically 'where's your car, Debbie, Debbie where's your car.'

'The man is obviously having some sort of breakdown,' says Betty. Betty was a psychiatric nurse. She tends to view everything from a mental health viewpoint.

Rather than coming to his assistance, though, everyone in the crowd is treating his existential crisis as an excuse to leap up and down. Why are they celebrating his sorry plight? What has happened to compassion?

'Debbie must surely be in the crowd somewhere,' I say. 'Why isn't she helping?'

'Where's your car, Debbie, Debbie where's your car.' the man screams over and over.

'Look at him. The poor man is at his wits end,' says Betty

'What make of car do you think it is?' I say. 'A Ford perhaps, or a Vauxhall? A Nissan or a Toyota? If we knew, Betty, we might be able to help. We might have seen it on the way here.'

'It would, of course, be helpful to know who Debbie is,' says Betty.

'For sure,' I say, looking around to see if there are any likely candidates. There are no obvious Debbies.

'I expect the poor man's life-saving drugs are in the car or something and he needs them,' Betty says. 'What on earth is Debbie thinking?'

'Of course, the pair of them might just be trying to get a lift home.' I say. 'And Debbie whoever she is doesn't want to give them a lift. She doesn't go that way or perhaps she hasn't got any petrol.'

Betty tells me I can be a bit cynical at times. She says I am unfeeling. But I think I have a point. The man cracking up over there seems to be a bit of an attention seeker. And now he has got his audience.

'You could be right,' Betty says, as we edge closer. 'They don't look like they are from round here, do they, Bill?'

'You don't think it might be some kind of ....... street theatre do you,' I say. 'Look. ....... There's a name on the drum. It says *Slaves.'*

'You not heard of *Slaves*, man,' says the youth spilling *Tennents Super* down his ripped vest. He lurches towards me. '*Slaves* is big, man. You wanna look out for them. They'll be headlining Glastonbury soon. That's where you old folks go, innit. Glastonbury. Look out for *Slaves*.'

# DRUGS

We are lounging in the garden of Astral Parlour, the name we have given to a pair of crumbling farm cottages deep in the Cotswold Hills. It is a summer afternoon and the sun is high overhead. There are about a dozen of us. I can't say for sure which of us are supposed to be living there and which of us are just hanging out, but we have temporarily taken over the cottages. I can't remember who made the arrangement, but I think they said we would do a few repairs and a bit of painting in return for accommodation. At eighteen, I believe I am the youngest, although no-one here is much over twenty five.

We are drinking jasmine tea, at least I think that's what it is, although Nathan Chillum was round cooking up some datura earlier. Nathan's something of a herbalist. Datura is used in ceremonies in the east. It has hallucinogenic properties. Anything with hallucinogenic properties seems to be welcome at Astral Parlour. Zero, the mad Jack Russell that someone here has adopted is running round, frantically chasing her tail. I wonder whether she has had some of Nathan's brew.

Meanwhile, the chocolate has run out. Someone needs to go and get some. No-one wants to drive the old grey A35 van the two miles to the filling station. It has no tax, no MOT and no number plates, and besides, everyone is too stoned. Quinn has been rolling joints all afternoon. I don't know much about the geography of dope cultivation but he said it was Nepalese temple balls or something. I've noticed that my friends tend to make a big deal out of the origin of what we are smoking. There is a strict hierarchy and Nepal is near the top along with Afghanistan and Kashmir.

Everything around here is kind of strange lately. Things haven't been the same around here since those purple tabs. They were a thousand mics, whatever that means. We were up for days.

Dewi is telling us about the brain police.

'When we were busy on that stuff last week,' he says. 'That's when the brain police came to visit.'

He is making us listen to *Burnt Weeny Sandwich* – again, in case there are some subliminal messages that he hasn't picked up on. I didn't realise it, but subliminal messages are everywhere, not just in television and advertising. A secret alliance of top people is trying to control our thoughts, we just don't realise it. Frank Zappa must be one of these.

Dewi comes from a remote village in Wales, whose name I cannot pronounce. I don't think the folks around there get out a lot. I can't remember how Dewi arrived here. First thing I can remember he came at me with his hair swinging wildly and thrust *Babylon* by Doctor John The Night Tripper at me and said, have you heard this, man, it's far out. Marianne thinks Dewi may have arrived in a spaceship. She could be right. He is always telling us about the UFO sightings in Wales.

I'm fed up of listening to the Mothers Of Invention and Captain Beefheart and his Magic Band. *Weasels Ripped My Flesh* and *Trout Mask Replica* are both complete nonsense. To be honest I liked it better when Mike was still here and we had *Pink Floyd* and *King Crimson*. Mike shouldn't have been arrested. It wasn't him who shot the Major's pig. It was Chadwick Dial. With his shotgun. Chad is a freak in the true sense of the word. He has a Quasimodo stoop and random strands of matted hair coming out from all corners of his head punctuated by random gaps. He can only see out of one eye, but the other one follows it around like a lost dog.

We used to have all kinds of people over when Mike was around. He was well connected. We had some circus folk for a while, a magic show came to stay and a theatre troupe used to drop by. Steve and Jimmy from *Traffic* came over one time and brought Quinn a guitar. Quinn doesn't play it anymore. He just rolls spliffs all day long and stares at the silhouette of the tree that is shaped like a tap against the western sky.

What is happening? …….. I'm being buffeted in time and space. ………. Waves of consciousness are coming through the static. Where am I? Who am I? …….. I am he and he is me, or something like that. …….. I wonder who can be writing this. …….. Here we go again.

Is it a decade later? It seems to be. Dewi is now living back in Wales. Another place with an unpronounceable name. He comes up to the Cotswolds on a visit. He happens by sheer chance to run into Chadwick Dial in *The Frog and Nightgown*. At closing time after several pints, Chadwick Dial, never one to miss an opportunity gets Dewi to give him a lift to a house party on the other side of town. Dewi has some coke and Chad helps him get through this. The two of them get into an argument over a girl Dewi is making a move on, a friend of Marianne's he says. By this time, everyone is well bashed and the argument quickly gets out of control. Dewi goes to leave, but Chad and some other revellers, who see him as a stranger, stop him in his tracks. At Chad's instigation they begin jumping up and down on the bonnet of his Sunbeam Alpine.

Dewi eventually manages to get them off. He does a swift hairpin turn and puts his foot down for a quick getaway. It could be that they have changed the priorities since he lived in these parts but he manages to go the wrong way down a one-way street. He does not know where he is. He finds himself heading out of town in the wrong direction. He is heading towards Stroud. His erratic driving draws the attention of a police patrol. They give chase, sirens wailing and blue lights flashing. Dewi tries to shake them off. Unable to control the powerful car on a bend Dewi ends up driving into a stone wall. He dies on impact.

As I make my way up the M5 from Bath I am hoping that I do not suffer a similar fate. It is three a.m. and I am driving an old Austin Maxi with Nathan Chillum as a passenger. We are being tailed by a jam sandwich patrol car. I am well over the drink drive limit and the car is full of cocaine. The bastards are following me at a distance of about twenty feet with their headlights on full beam. There are no other cars on the road so it is quite clear that they are just trying to intimidate me, trying to make me wonder when they are going to pull me over. I am nervous about night driving at the best of times, but the day's intake of drink and drugs turns this into a state of blind panic. My feet are shaking on the pedals. I am gibbering. Nathan too is gibbering. I can already hear prison doors slam behind me.

I approach my exit. It is do or die. Will they follow me or will they carry on up the motorway? With the headlights nearly blinding me, I miss the turn-off from the exit road and find myself back on the motorway still heading north. I realise the game is up. The police are still behind me. They put the sirens on and pull me over. Nathan and I get out. We have to put as much distance between the police and the cocaine as possible.

Nathan mitigates my blunder by saying, 'the lights, man, you were blinding him.'

Nathan looks out of his head even when he is not, which is seldom. I don't feel he is helping my case.'

The officer with the night driving glasses goes through the routine of, is this your car, what's the registration number, have you been drinking, to which I manage to give the right answers.

'We'd turn you over,' says the other officer, the senior of the two. 'But we can't be bothered tonight. It would mean too much paperwork. And you've probably only got enough hash for a joint or two. But get your tail light fixed before you go on the motorway at night again.'

The scene is fading. I feel like I'm swimming in the sea and I see people on the shore, but they're getting farther and farther away. ...... Wait! ........ The atmospheric radio is retuning. ...... Where are we now? ........ Ah! I don't think I like this one. Why am I here? ..... Can someone get me out of here!

They'll never find it. They'll never find it. I am willing them not to find it. It's not that well hidden, but they've been searching the flat for an hour now. Will they find it? There's seventeen ounces there. Behind the water tank, wedged against the wall. It's a sizeable stretch for me if they do find it. They must have been tipped off. There would have been a fraction of this amount only yesterday.

I try to think of who might have grassed me up. The Welsh rugby playing next door neighbour with the dogs? He will have witnessed all the comings and goings? That little jerk that hangs around with Brad? The gopher who sits around in his BMW while he does his business. The woman I was seeing last year, what was her name? Cheryl, Cherry, Shelley? Perhaps these drug squad guys have been sitting in a car outside for days watching me. No, surely I would have noticed. Perhaps they have been following me.

They are going through my personal things, my unpublished stories, the candid photos I took of Saskia, the letters that I did not send. D.S. Bowser is telling me that they nearly got me three months ago when they raided Saskia's. I remember it well. About a dozen of them in blue fatigues burst in, but they did not know what they were looking for. All they got was a cannabis plant in the greenhouse. The officers concerned did not realise who I was until recently, D.S. Bowser says.

I am going to have to go down to the station anyway, because of what they found in the cupboard. It was only a gram or so of billy, but I can't imagine they'll overlook it.

'Can you get someone to look after your daughter?' Bowser asks. 'She's a bit young for police cells.'

Does this mean they are about to give up the search? Settle for what they've got? I wonder who it is best to phone. I phone Saskia. She is not there, so I leave a message in such a way that she knows what's going on. She may need to let others know not to call in. Just in case.

'Come here Sarge!' says an excited voice.

I instinctively know that the game is up. They have found it.


Is that it? ........ Is that all there is? I feel woozy. ......... Have I been asleep? ........ Unconscious?...... Where am I? There are tubes and cath.... What do they call those things they put in your arm? I can't get a handle on anything. It must be the drugs. .......... I think I may be coming round from ...... From what? I can smell formaldehyde ........... I hope the ............ procedure was a ........ a success.

# Chinese Boxes

The fire engine comes hurtling towards me. It is out of control. It has no driver. Conan Doyle Street is narrow and the precipitate leviathan gathers momentum as it heads down the slope. I dive for safety into the doorway of the antiquarian bookstore. The fire engine forges ahead, gradually slowing as the incline levels out. It comes to a stop in the dip where Conan Doyle Street meets Rider Haggard Street. Fortunately, there are no casualties as the streets are deserted. This part of town is no longer prosperous and a lot of the shops are boarded up.

I am on my way to the doctor's in Bram Stoker Street, a block or so away. I don't have an appointment, but when I phoned earlier I was told someone would see me if I came along. I let the sour faced receptionist know of my arrival and sit in the grey waiting room. Afternoon surgery has finished and I am the only one there. For comfort, I take my *Doc Martens* off. I start to read a monthly military magazine, but I can't concentrate. After a few minutes, Dr Bilk comes through and says that he will see me but he has to make a phonecall to the hospital first. He asks me to go wait for him in Surgery 2.

Realising I am in stockinged feet, I go back to fetch my boots. It takes a while to lace them up and when I return Surgery 2 is locked. Dr Bilk has disappeared. I look everywhere for him. I go out into the court-yard. I look up and down the street. Back inside, a dozen or so men in dark suits are having a meeting in the room down the corridor from the locked surgery. There is a hostile air about the gathering. I do not like to interrupt. I go out to the car park. I manage to collar Dr Bilk, just as he is getting into his car. Without bothering to listen to my symptoms, he hurriedly writes me a prescription. I have not heard of the medication, he prescribes. Perhaps he has made a mistake.

What makes me want to return the fire engine to the fire station I do not know. This is what happens sometimes, isn't it? In a moment of madness you find you make a decision that you just can't account for. It's as if a force takes over and you no longer have free will. It may be just me but I have noticed that these decisions are often injudicious.

I am not used to handling such a bulky vehicle and I have several near collisions with other cars on the way. I accidentally cross two sets of red traffic lights and manage to negotiate the Henry James roundabout on two wheels. When I finally arrive at the firestation, I find that it is closed. What would happen if there were a fire? I park the vehicle outside the book depository in Franz Kafka Street. I think about phoning my brother, Quinn to come and pick me up, as it is now after six o'clock and I need to get home for dinner. I am suddenly struck by the thought that my fingerprints will be all over the fire engine and they will think that it was me that stole it.

I come to with a start. I do not recognise my surroundings. Red would not be everyone's choice of colour for bedroom walls and Francis Bacon's *mutilated torso* prints would not be to everyone's taste to hang on them. There is a large sagging woollen drape coming down from the ceiling and a silver saxophone on a stand in the corner of the room, alongside a device that looks like a medieval instrument of torture. *Mr Bojangles* is playing from a portable red speaker, a grunge version that I am not familiar with. The room has a musty smell.

The important question seems to me to be how did I come to be here? I have no recollection. Where is my beautiful house, my beautiful wife and my large automobile? How do I work this? Before I have a chance to get my bearings there is a loud knock at the door. I leave it at first, but when no-one else answers it, I conclude that I must be alone here. On the second or third knock, I go to to the door. A man is standing there holding a large metal plate. He doesn't seem surprised to see me.

'I've come to fix the cooker,' he says.

'You'd better come in.' I say.

I don't have any idea where the kitchen is, but he seems to know.

'Did I wake you up?' he asks, as I follow him through to the kitchen.

'No,' I say, looking around to take in the funky chickens strutting about the place.

'Good idea to keep them indoors,' Cookerman says. 'Stops the foxes getting them. There are a lot of foxes about round here.'

I don't ask him where round here is in case he gets suspicious.

'Rhode Island Reds, these little beauties,' he says. 'Good for laying brown eggs. Perhaps we might have breakfast when I've done the cooker.'

The kitchen is kitted out in an odd mix of styles, a startling hybrid of Scandinavian chic and Dickensian squalor. I have not seen a zebra patterned fridge, or a red cooker before. Cookerman takes it all in his stride. Perhaps he comes across vibrant appliances every day. Ducking beneath the cast iron pots and pans hanging from butcher's hooks on the ceiling, he makes his way over to the cooker and opens the door. I don't know if you've ever seen a cooker explode. I'm guessing most of you haven't. But I can tell you, it does wake you up.

Which is how I come to find myself in a barnacled beach hut in the middle of a storm surge, with the waters already sloshing over the sandbags. The wind is getting up again and it has turned round to the north. The spring tide is due to keep coming in for the next two hours. Looking through the gap where the window once was I can see more black clouds forming over the steep escarpment the other side of the bay. With the water already around our ankles and the roof leaking like a faucet, the last thing we need is another downpour.

Earlier, I tried in vain to rescue a struggling black Labrador that was being taken away by the rip current. My leg became trapped and I was thrown against the rocks. I was knocked unconscious. She is only slight and I am nearly fourteen stone but somehow Vision dragged me here to this beach hut, the highest beach hut in the row. Some of the other huts have already broken to pieces and been taken out to sea. I can hardly move my damaged leg, so we won't be leaving anytime soon. We are at the mercy of the elements. We are trapped.

'Don't you know what time high water is?' Vision asks, looking at her watch. 'It must be soon.'

'14:05. Nearly two hours to go.'

'We can't stay here that long. We'll drown.'

'We'll send out a mayday then, shall we? Where did you put the flares?'

'I could go for help,' she says.

We are caught between the devil and the deep blue sea. If Vision goes for help we are both at risk. If she stays we are still both at risk.

'No,' I say, with some authority. 'Don't go.'

'I guess we're in this together then,' she says. 'That's what we used to say isn't it?'

'It's been a long time,' I say. 'Seven years, isn't it? Or is it nine?'

'Twelve, I think,' she says.

As the waves continue to crash against the flimsy fabric of the hut, it feels like being aboard a ship going down. I have the urge to break into a sea shanty, to summon up the sailor's spirit, *Blow The Man Down, Haul Away Joe* or something like that.

Is that a lifeboat I can see in the distance? ....... Is it? ....... Or is it just another phantom? Am I doomed perhaps to an endless chain of unfathomable nightmares from which I can never wake? Doomed to grapple feebly with this nest of interlocking riddles, that fit inside one another like Chinese boxes?

17785297R00094

Printed in Poland
by Amazon Fulfillment
Poland Sp. z o.o., Wrocław